The Eucharist

A Story about What Matters

Pamela J Peck

Order this book online at www.trafford.com/07-1134
or email orders@trafford.com

Most Trafford titles are also available at major online book retailers.

© Copyright 2008 Pamela J. Peck.

All rights reserved. No part of this publication may be reproduced, stored in a retrieval system, or transmitted, in any form or by any means, electronic, mechanical, photocopying, recording, or otherwise, without the written prior permission of the author.

Illustrated by Pamela J Peck
Edited by Ken Johson, MJ
Cover design/Artwork by Pamela J Peck
Layout and design by PJenesis Press

Note for Librarians: A cataloguing record for this book is available from Library and Archives Canada at www.collectionscanada.ca/amicus/index-e.html

Printed in Victoria, BC, Canada.

ISBN: 978-1-4251-3102-9

We at Trafford believe that it is the responsibility of us all, as both individuals and corporations, to make choices that are environmentally and socially sound. You, in turn, are supporting this responsible conduct each time you purchase a Trafford book, or make use of our publishing services. To find out how you are helping, please visit www.trafford.com/responsiblepublishing.html

Our mission is to efficiently provide the world's finest, most comprehensive book publishing service, enabling every author to experience success. To find out how to publish your book, your way, and have it available worldwide, visit us online at www.trafford.com/10510

www.trafford.com

North America & international
toll-free: 1 888 232 4444 (USA & Canada)
phone: 250 383 6864 ♦ fax: 250 383 6804
email: info@trafford.com

The United Kingdom & Europe
phone: +44 (0)1865 722 113 ♦ local rate: 0845 230 9601
facsimile: +44 (0)1865 722 868 ♦ email: info.uk@trafford.com

10 9 8 7 6 5 4 3

To the spirit in all of us

The Eucharist

PROLOGUE

In the Beginning

No one in this rather ordinary English country town could have imagined so miraculous an event taking place right before their eyes. It didn't happen all at once, of course. Like the rhythms of nature, the mysterious workings took time to root, to blossom and grow. It all began many years ago, when an ambitious young man named Wilbur Spencer bought a piece of prime real estate in the centre of town and created the Spencer Department Store.

Over the years, the venture proved successful and provided a very comfortable living for the man and his family. One could say he enjoyed "the good life", and he was an astute businessman in more ways than one. By the time he reached middle age, he had positioned himself well enough to control not only his commercial venture but the banking institution of the town as well.

More years passed. Then, in spite of his wealth and prominence, something happened that caused the man to become introspective. In the midst of his solitude, he made the biggest purchase of his life: a full square block of real estate adjacent to the Spencer Department Store on Main Street. The townsfolk could be excused for believing he would extend his financial interests on this coveted piece of property. Why else would one make so monumental an investment so late in life?

But the man surprised everyone by building . . . not a store . . . not an office . . . not a bank . . . . No, this time he built . . . a cathedral.

The Mother of Sorrow Cathedral. Why? He was not a religious man by any means. And the town already had an Anglican church. The old man explained to no one why he had built it. But it was clear to everyone it was very dear to his heart.

By the time he reached a respectable old age, the man had accumulated a sizable fortune both in land and money, a state of affairs that should have made his two adult sons very happy. But happiness eluded them. Not because money—or land, for that matter—didn't please them. On the contrary, it was because both sons aspired to control the family empire when their father died and, as a result, they became very jealous of each other.

Family discord the old man could not abide. For some profound unspoken reason, he determined to use his wealth to keep them together rather than tear them apart. But in spite of his best efforts, he could not mend the rift between them.

Life, however, had taught the old man a powerful if not painful lesson: sometimes in death one can achieve what cannot be accomplished in life. From that wisdom he crafted a solution. He set up his will in such a way that the two brothers must cooperate in order to benefit from their inheritance. To the older son he left all his money but no land on which to build. To the younger, he gave all his land but no money with which to develop it. Neither the money nor the land could be used by the one without the consent of the other. And the conditions of the will would apply to all succeeding generations.

The two sons married and established families of their own. To the first son, twin daughters were born, named, at the request of their grandfather, Catherine and Dolores. To the second was born only one son who died soon after his own infant son was born. The infant was named Wilbur in honour of his great-grandfather. Soon thereafter the old man departed from the world, and the mystery of the cathedral was buried with him.

The years passed. The identical twins blossomed into womanhood, and have now reached the healthy age of "three score year and ten". They never married. As a result, they produced no offspring to inherit the fortune bequeathed to them through the Spencer family line.

Unlike his spinster aunties, Wilbur did marry, but like his great uncle, he produced no sons. Instead, he is now the not-so-proud father of three daughters, all but one, at this critical point in time, too young to enter into legal or financial negotiations with elderly identical twins who are not at all keen to do business with Wilbur. And the oldest daughter, Jenny, the only one of legal age, shares none of her father's interest in commerce.

No joint venture, no access to the fistful of capital stashed away in a shoebox in the home of a pair of elderly identical twins. In short, the Spencer family fortune is threatened with dissolution. Threatened, that is, unless Wilbur can come up with a plan.

It's all about miracles.

CHAPTER I

Wilbur and the Twins

The Mother of Sorrow Cathedral, in its park-like setting of Cathedral Square, dominates the centre of the English country town. On this mid-December afternoon, a soft snow is falling. Christmas lights twinkle in the Square and along Main Street. Shoppers, arms filled with packages, scurry about exchanging Christmas cheer. A Santa, wearing a kilt, collects money for the poor as the bells of the Cathedral chime.

Next to Cathedral Park is the prominent Spencer Department Store, owned and operated by Wilbur and his elderly identical twin aunts. Next to the Department Store is the town's only bank, a two-storey structure of wood and stone where Wilbur, as joint owner and bank manager, keeps his office on the second floor.

On this occasion, Arnold, a nattily dressed banking clerk in his mid-twenties stands outside the front door of the bank. Four delinquent boys discover him there and start harassing him. Arnold is an easy target; he is overweight, wears thick glasses — and speaks with a lisp.

The boys razz and poke fun at him. Arnold tries to fend them off but he is no match for their pitiless jibes.

Ah, but relief is in sight. Catherine and Dolores Spencer, 70-year-old identical twins, stride deliberately toward the bank. They are in a no-nonsense mood.

Catherine and Dolores are identical in every sense of the word. They look alike—and dress alike. They have identical mannerisms, even identical expressions. It is apparent now that Arnold has been waiting for them. When the delinquent boys see the twins approaching, they instantly back off. Relieved at last, Arnold greets the twins and escorts them into the bank.

Along the street in the opposite direction, another pair of sisters is heading for the bank. But in this case, it's the *young* Spencers. Priscilla is seventeen—going on twenty-five—and her sister Angelina is a precocious ten-year-old. In contrast to their great aunties, these girls are in a festive mood. When they get to the bank, they don't go inside. Instead, they gather up snow, pack it into snowballs, and toss them at a second storey window, giggling as they brush themselves off. Their father, Wilbur, ripe for a mid-life crisis, appears at the window. He looks down and sees them, slides opens the wood-frame window and grins.

"Mom says don't be late," yells Priscilla, before her father has a chance to speak. "Jenny's train gets in at 6:20."

THE EUCHARIST

"I'll try," responds her father. "I have an important meeting."

"Daddy, you've got to be there," states his daughter emphatically. "It's her homecoming."

"I know, Priscilla, but I'm very busy," comes his reply.

"But I'm very busy," Angelina mocks, in a voice too low for her father to hear. Then she shouts up to him, "Hi Daddy!"

"Hi, Angel," he responds.

Wilbur waves and closes the window. Priscilla and Angelina try to wave back. Too late! He has disappeared.

Inside the office, architectural drawings are spread across a large wooden desk. The elderly twins enter, ushered in by Arnold. Wilbur greets them as he moves away from the window.

"Aunties, come right in," says Wilbur, smiling at them. "How are we today?" He cozies up to them.

Arnold stands there, watching. Wilbur waves him away. It takes Arnold a moment to catch on; he leaves.

Wilbur directs the twins to the drawings on his desk. "Come see, the plans are all drawn up. It'll be the biggest commercial venture this town has ever seen. Grand-dad would be so proud."

Catherine and Dolores peer at the architectural drawings. Their gestures and expressions are, as usual, identical.

"How much money, nephew?" asks Catherine.

"How much money, nephew?" repeats Dolores.

Wilbur presses the intercom button on his desk. "Arnold, would you bring in the figures." Immediately, there is a vigorous knock on the door.

"Come in, Arnold," says Wilbur.

Arnold enters, carrying a pile of papers. "Here they are, thir. I thet them up juth the way you wanted. The inithal outlay, projected cothts, the payment thedule and the—"

"Good, Arnold," says Wilbur. "You can leave them with me."

"Yeth, thir, and if you need me, I'll be—"

"That'll be all for now, Arnold."

"Okay, thir." Arnold turns to go, then stops. "Ith Jenny coming home for Chrithmath, thir?"

Wilbur is absorbed in thought, preparing to show his aunts the paperwork. "Yes she is, Arnold," he answers, without raising his head. "She arrives today." Arnold's nervousness disappears for a moment and he breaks out in a wide grin. He just stands there. Wilbur looks up at him. "You can go now, Arnold."

Arnold comes back to reality. "Ah, yeth, thank-you, thir. Bye, Thpenther thithters."

Catherine and Dolores peer at Arnold as he clumsily leaves the room.

CHAPTER II

Michael and the Verger

While Wilbur is busy selling the elderly twins on a commercial venture inside his second storey bank office, down the street, at the Mother of Sorrow Cathedral, preparations are underway for the Christmas season. In one sense, it looks like Christmas every day at the Cathedral because its prominent feature is a beautiful stained glass window of a Madonna-like mother and child, positioned high and in the very centre of a most stunning piece of architecture.

This is not to say that all is well at the Cathedral. Quite the contrary. For in front of the building, beside the bold "Mother of Sorrow Cathedral" lettering stands a second sign,—a temporary one—that reads "Save the Cathedral. Support the Restoration Fund". Beside the sign is a barometer indicating the fund-raising effort has reached only the one-quarter mark.

But right now thoughts are elsewhere: it is Christmas and they are decorating big time. It falls to the seventy-two year old Verger to make sure things get done the way they should be done; that is to say, the way the Dean wants them done. The Verger is tall and slim and rather tired looking, but he has a distinct air of strength and authenticity about him. Right now he is setting up an outdoor nativity scene, and emerges from the Cathedral carrying a statuette of the Mother Mary.

With the Verger, on this occasion, is Father Michael Anthony, a priest newly appointed to the Cathedral. Michael is 24 years old, handsome and very energetic. Mother of Sorrow Cathedral is his first posting and he is eager to learn the ropes. He follows behind the Verger, carrying a cradle that holds the baby Jesus.

The two men walk to the edge of the Cathedral grounds, sheltered by a high stone wall. The Verger positions the statuette of Mary, then pauses and looks intently at it. "Ah, dear Mother," he says to her gently, "do I detect a sadness in your face? What's the trouble? Cheer up. Look, we've brought you your little miracle." He taps her cheek. Then he gets up as Michael sets the cradle with the infant Jesus in place.

The Verger moves a few steps and tugs on a rope attached to a bell mounted on top of the wall. There is no sound. "It's stuck," he says. "I'll have to get a ladder and loosen it." Michael looks at it, reaches for a handful of snow, forms a snowball and hurls it toward the bell.

Gong! It's a bullseye!

THE EUCHARIST

The Verger tugs at the rope again. This time the bell rings! He looks at Michael. "Pretty good aim, Father!" he says.

Michael dismisses his achievement with a wave of his hand and turns to leave. "Call me Michael," he says to the Verger as he heads toward the street.

"Thanks for your help . . . Michael," the Verger calls after him. Without turning to look back, the young priest acknowledges the Verger by waving his arm.

CHAPTER III

The Dean and Mrs. Pebblebaum

The Verger walks back toward the Cathedral. From outside he can hear the sound of children singing.

Jesus was a little child
Born into a manger
There he lay so meek and mild
To the world a stranger

The Verger steps inside. Mrs. Loretta Pebblebaum, a full-figured woman in her forties and wife of the town's prominent lawyer, is rehearsing a children's choir for the upcoming Christmas pageant. The pageant is especially important this year, as it will double as a fundraiser for repair of the Cathedral.

Shepherds keeping watch at night
In the fields abiding
Saw the heavens fill with light
Heard the angel tiding

The Verger pauses to listen to the children singing.

Wise men journey from afar
Precious gifts they carry
Guided by a wondrous star
To the mother Mary

Peace on Earth from God above
Hear the angel voices
Jesus is the Lord of love
All the world rejoices

"Okay, stop a minute!" shouts Mrs. Pebblebaum as she struts over to the organ and gives the organist some instructions.

Dean Potts wanders into the sanctuary. A cleric in his early fifties, the Dean is slightly less than medium height, is rather round and has a pinkish complexion. The Dean is of "the old school"; put another way, there is only one way to do things—his way!

"Ah, there you are, Verger," says the Dean. "Tree has arrived." He points to a large Christmas tree leaning against the communion rail. The Verger takes the tree and positions it off to one side.

"No, I don't think we'll put it there this year," states the Dean. He points to the opposite wall. "There . . . put it over there."

THE EUCHARIST

The Verger moves to comply without question or expression. One can tell he has learned to do what he is told even when it goes against his better judgment. He slides the tree to the opposite side of the sanctuary.

"Okay, last verse," pipes up Mrs. Pebblebaum. "A little slower and more volume."

The children sing.

Christ the king was born for us
Lift your voice in singing
Hallelujah, glorious
Christmas bells are ringing

"Very nice, Mrs. Pebblebaum," mouths the Dean without expression.

"Oh, thank-you very much, Dean," responds Mrs. Pebblebaum, flattered by the compliment.

The Dean's attention has already shifted as he heads to his office. Mrs. Pebblebaum stares after him. "But it's the children who deserve the praise . . . their charming little voices."

"Charming," repeats the Dean, once more without expression.

Mrs. Pebblebaum tries again. "Oh, I brought you your favourite pick-me-up," she declares gleefully as she descends from the choir loft with a cookie tin.

Dean Potts stops and perks up. "Oh, well, I guess," he says giggling. "After all, it's Christmas." He returns to the centre of the sanctuary.

Mrs. Pebblebaum beams with delight. "Got to keep you jolly!" she pronounces enthusiastically as she opens the tin and thrusts it in front of him. "Take two; they're small!" she giggles.

Dean Potts helps himself to the sweets as the Verger watches with quiet amusement.

CHAPTER IV

Wilbur and the Lawyer

The stenciled printing on the glass window in the door spells out "Samuel Pebblebaum, Legal Counsel". Inside, Wilbur sits across the desk from his lawyer who is examining a file of legal documents.

"No, that's a necessary step," states Samuel. "The will clearly states you must give them the option. It's their land 'so long as the church shall stand'. With the proviso that, quote, 'it be in regular use and properly maintained'."

"So if they don't raise the funds to repair it . . ." Wilbur probes.

"The lease can be cancelled at year's end," Samuel replies.

"Of this year?" Wilbur wants to confirm.

"Of *any* year," replies his lawyer. "The will simply states it be at the end of a calendar year."

"And I don't have to give them more time to raise the money?" Wilbur asks.

"It's an oversight in the will, I dare say," Samuel confirms, "but that's the way it's written. You are simply required to serve notice that you are not extending the lease."

"So . . . three weeks," says Wilbur.

"Whew!" the lawyer exclaims. "Doesn't give them much time . . . but . . . it's legal."

Wilbur pauses a moment and sits back in his chair. "So when can you have it ready?"

"The notice? One day. It can be served tomorrow," replies his lawyer.

"Okay . . . good," Wilbur replies.

Samuel checks through the papers in the file. "Now, all this has the approval of your aunts?"

Wilbur makes no comment.

Samuel looks up from his reading. "I take it they're in full agreement?" he questions.

Wilbur is evasive. "I've gone over the plans with them in detail."

"And they're prepared to bankroll the lot?" Samuel queries.

"They've seen the numbers," Wilbur answers.

"Well then," Samuel states, "you're on your way."

"Under the new company name," Wilbur adds.

The lawyer glances back at the file and reads. "GEM Enterprises . . . or is it G-E-M?"

THE EUCHARIST

Wilbur avoids the question and changes the subject. "Now, because they have no children, the spinsters . . . ah . . . the inheritance when they . . . you know, after they are . . ." He doesn't come right out and say it.

"In legal terms, where there is no issue," the lawyer states with certainty, "whatever monies are still held by them revert to the state."

"So it's wise for me to get them to invest all of it," Wilbur adds.

"Legally . . . and financially," Samuel confirms, "it's a good move for you."

"And the total revenue will be mine when . . . you know, after they . . ." Wilbur tries to pose the question delicately.

"According to the will," says Samuel, "so long as the money is tied up in your land, it's legally yours."

"So that's all I need to do?" Wilbur asks again.

"All you need to do," Samuel confirms.

Wilbur pushes his chair away from the desk. He stands up, leans across the desk and shakes hands with his lawyer.

CHAPTER V

Verger and the Officer

The Verger emerges from the front door of the Cathedral and turns a spotlight on the crèche. He kneels down and rearranges the infant in the cradle. Nearby, the four delinquent boys who were harassing Arnold are pelting the "Save the Cathedral" sign with snowballs. A police officer runs toward them. "Hey, you punks," he shouts at them.

The Verger looks up. The boys start to run away. "Freeze! Right there!" the policeman continues.

The boys stop. The officer approaches them. "I'm taking you in! Defacing church property!"

The Verger approaches them as the policeman snaps handcuffs. "Is it just a matter of the sign, Officer?" asks the Verger.

"No, sir," he replies, "they've been stirrin' up trouble all over town. People have been complaining about this gang for—"

"They're only children, sir," the Verger states. "They just need something to do."

"Oh, we'll give 'em somethin' to do, alright," the officer replies.

"They're not hurting anything," the Verger tries to reason.

"This here is a clear case of malicious and intentional property damage," the policeman insists.

"It's just a sign, sir. Let them hit it. Saves the stained-glass windows. You know how children are. Probably have some of your own."

"What you're tellin' me, sir," the policeman states, resting his hands on his hips, "is that the church grants permission for these punks to destroy that sign?"

"They have permission to snowball it," the Verger replies.

The officer removes the handcuffs. "Okay, Verger, I have a feeling I'm the one being snowballed here. But if you're assuming responsibility for this damage, they're all yours." He turns to the boys. "Just keep off the street, hear me? 'Cause if I catch you out here one more time, I'm gonna book you good." He struts away.

The Verger and the boys look at the damaged sign. "Pretty good aim," states the Verger.

The boys laugh nervously.

"There's a guy here who can hit the bell on top of that wall," the Verger continues. He points to the stone wall beyond the crèche that defines the border of Cathedral Park. The boys look up.

THE EUCHARIST

"Not bad, eh?" says the Verger. He looks at the boys. "Can you aim that high?"

The boys shrug.

"I hear he plays guitar, too," the Verger continues.

The boys perk up. "He got any drums?" one of them asks.

"I think so," the Verger replies. "Why don't you come by tomorrow. He'll be here."

The boys look at each other but say nothing.

The Verger speaks more gently. "Okay, off you go now. And, ah . . . better stay off the street." He nods at them with a twinkle in his eye.

The boys retreat a few steps, then, as if on cue, reach down for snow, pack it, and take aim at the bell on top of the wall. None is on target.

The Verger watches the boys saunter down the street. The scene reminds him of a poem he wrote about children a long time ago. The words come flooding back to him now.

Are seeds of hatred planted in the ground
They must be planted somewhere
'Cause they flourish all around
Do grown-ups know the reason
Is the answer in the sky
Oh, how long will children keep on asking why

Free the children now, oh, help their eyes to see
Love and kindness now instead of apathy
Heaven knows I try when they look up to me
'Cause it's what they see today they do tomorrow

"Yes," the Verger muses, "it's what they see today they do tomorrow." He turns and walks back inside the Cathedral.

CHAPTER VI

Wilbur and His Daughter

Wilbur does finish his meeting in time to be at the train station. He stands now on the platform beside Margaret, a petit woman in her early forties who has very good taste, one befitting her social role as wife of the bank manager, and key member of the wealthiest and most influential family in town. Motherhood is important to her too. And right now she waits with anticipation for the arrival of their eldest daughter, Jenny. Priscilla and Angelina are also here to greet their sister.

"Oh, Wilbur," says Margaret, "it's so exciting, having her home for Christmas. Wonder what she's learned. She'll have so much to tell."

"Should be taking commerce," her husband replies without expression.

"Wouldn't suit her, dear. She's esoteric."

"She's impractical, that's what she is. Who's gonna hire her?" Wilbur retorts.

"Maybe she'll meet a rich man at college and never have to work," pipes up Priscilla. "That's what I'm gonna do."

"Jenny says she's never getting married," reminds Angelina.

The train whistle sounds in the distance. The family members beam with excitement—except for Wilbur, that is, who stands stalwart, his eyes staring off into space.

The train puffs into the station and grinds to a halt. A conductor jumps down from a coach and places a small portable step onto the platform. Soon the passengers begin to emerge. Spencer family members peer at the arrivals, looking for that one familiar face.

And there she is! Twenty-year-old Jenny steps into the doorway of a rail car, suitcase in hand. Jenny is tall and very slim, and is dressed in a fitted wool coat and scarf. She gazes along the platform.

Priscilla and Angelina spot her. "Jenny! Jenny!" shout her sisters in unison as they run toward her.

"Priscilla! Angel!" Jenny shouts back. She steps from the train and runs along the platform toward them. They meet and embrace, then move together, arm in arm, to where their parents are standing.

"Mom! Dad! Oh, it's good to be home," says Jenny as she embraces them. "I missed all of you."

"I'm gonna be in a pageant, Jenny," offers Angelina, excitedly.

THE EUCHARIST

"That's wonderful, Angel."

"Father Anthony's doing it," Angelina continues.

"Slow down, Angel," exclaims Jenny. "Who's Father Anthony?"

"Oh, he's the new priest at the Cathedral, dear," says Margaret. "He's very nice."

"And really handsome," adds Angelina.

"Jenny's never gonna getting married, remember?" interjects Priscilla.

"Well, she doesn't have to *marry* him," pronounces Angelina.

"Hush, Angel," says her mother. Then she turns to Jenny. "He's just getting started. You'll get a chance to meet him at the Christmas Tea. I've asked the Dean to bring him along."

"You haven't had the Tea yet?" exclaims Jenny.

"No, dear, I was waiting for you," replies Margaret.

"Oh, Mom, you know I don't like those things."

"And guess what!" Angelina tells her sister. "Daddy rigged up the doorbells again!"

"Oh, Mom, you're not going to do that sing-along thing, are you?" Jenny protests.

"Just at the beginning, dear," her mother responds, "to welcome the guests. They really enjoy it."

"Well, I think it's . . . well, never mind."

"And the girls are doing a classical number as usual," adds Margaret.

"Well, just so long as I don't have to do it again," Jenny sighs.

Wilbur picks up Jenny's suitcase in an attempt to get the group moving.

"Are there any rich men at college, Jenny?" asks Priscilla.

Jenny laughs. "I don't know, Priscilla. What's all this interest in men!" She takes her mother's arm as they leave the station.

CHAPTER VII

Verger and the Dean

Inside the Cathedral office, Dean Potts sits at his desk staring at the Notice of Lease Termination. The Verger stands just inside the doorway.

"How long do they give us?" asks the Verger.

"End of the year," replies the Dean.

"That's less than three weeks," responds the Verger. "It would take a miracle!"

Dean Potts stands up and saunters to the window. "Some people think that's the business we're in," he says sarcastically as he stares outside. "We would need to bring in at least fifty thousand by Christmas. Put that with what's left in the maintenance fund . . ."

"Not enough time, sir," the Verger responds in a calm voice.

Dean Potts returns to his desk and picks up the legal notice. "Who are they, anyway? GEM Enterprises . . . or is it G-E-M . . . ? Never heard of them."

"Old man Spencer would turn in his grave," says the Verger quietly.

"And just when we finally got the new priest," adds the Dean.

The Verger thinks for a moment. "What does Wilbur say, sir? It's his land."

"Bank needs the investment capital or it'll go under," the Dean replies. "And the developers won't settle for any other building site. Says he doesn't have a choice."

"Seems he would stand to gain if the Cathedral came down," suggests the Verger.

Dean Potts responds immediately. "Spencer's the pillar of this church. He'll look out for us."

"Of course, sir," the Verger replies, against his own better judgment.

"In fact," reveals the Dean, "he said he has already negotiated space for a sanctuary in the basement of the new complex."

"In the basement, sir?" the Verger clarifies.

"Yeah. Says they could design it so there'd be a beam of light coming down through the ceiling," the Dean continues.

The Verger is silent. After a few moments, he speaks. "Maybe it's the best plan, sir. Would get around all the maintenance problems."

"Well," replies the Dean, "just between you and me, that's what I'm beginning to think. But it would be a leaner, meaner . . . What I mean to say is, it would be a trimmed down church. The youth program would have to go and . . . about the maintenance . . . ah . . . well, the thing is, that would be taken care of by . . . ah . . . by the building complex. They would have their own people . . . which means we wouldn't have need of . . . There wouldn't be a position for . . . ummm . . ."

"Oh, don't you worry about me, sir," the Verger responds, helping the Dean out of a difficult situation.

"Well, it wouldn't be something I had control over, you understand," the Dean continues.

"I understand, sir."

There is a protracted silence — an ominous silence — as though the tearing down of the Cathedral is a foregone conclusion. At least the Dean seems to think that way because now he becomes rather animated. "You know, that beam of light," he says to the Verger, "it could shine right down on the altar. Wouldn't that be something!"

"It would, sir," replies the Verger quietly.

"And we could get one of those new round ones," adds the Dean.

"A round altar, sir?" questions the Verger.

"Yeah, it's the latest thing. People sitting in a circle." The Dean makes a circular formation with his arms.

"Ah," says the Verger. There is silence again.

"Yeah, I think a round one," the Dean muses now, almost talking to himself. The Verger stands quietly as the Dean becomes lost in thought.

"Will that be all, sir?" the Verger asks softly after a few moments have passed.

Dean Potts is jarred from his imagining. "Yes, yes. That's all for now."

"Thank-you, sir." The Verger turns to leave.

"Oh, and, ummm . . ." adds the Dean before the Verger can get through the doorway, "let's not mention this to anyone, shall we. It's not public knowledge yet."

"You have my word, sir," the Verger affirms as he quietly walks away.

CHAPTER VIII

Margaret and Her Daughter

Margaret is making her celebrated shortbread for the Christmas Tea. Jenny is with her, more or less helping but primarily enjoying time with her mother. Margaret rolls out the dough, stopping periodically to add flour to a large bowl of sugar and butter that Jenny is stirring.

"I love these shortbread," says Jenny.

"Tell me what you've learned, dear," Margaret asks her daughter.

"Well, mainly it just changes the way I see things," Jenny replies. "At first it's confusing. But then it all starts to come together."

"How do you mean, dear?" her mother asks.

"Well," replies Jenny, "like the idea that because of the way we think, we create problems we can't solve at the same level we created them at."

"Oh, that *is* confusing," acknowledges Margaret.

Jenny stops stirring. "And you know who said that?"

"Who, dear?"

"Einstein."

"Einstein? He wasn't a philosopher, was he?" her mother questions.

"No, but that's what I mean," says Jenny. "At some level it all starts to come together. But first you have to, I don't know, forget everything you ever learned, like in church and even from your parents."

Margaret laughs. "Oh, dear, I don't think your father would like to hear you say that!"

"Because to solve a problem," Jenny continues, "you have to create a new level of thinking."

Margaret cuts a strip of rolled dough and spreads the pieces evenly on a cookie sheet. "And how do you do that, dear?" she asks patiently.

"The way one of the professors put it is that you have to break the mind set," Jenny explains.

"You've lost me," says Margaret. She points to the bowl of cookie dough Jenny is supposed to be stirring. "Is that ready?"

Jenny resumes stirring as she explains further. "And he said that to ask is to break the set."

"Ask what, dear?" her mother wants to know.

"I don't know. Just ask, I guess," says Jenny. "Is Daddy still upset with me?"

"Oh, give him time, dear," advises her mother. "He just doesn't see a job in your future."

THE EUCHARIST

"My job is to work on myself," says Jenny with great confidence. "And whatever happens, happens."

Margaret puts her hands to her mouth and laughs. "Oh, dear! But don't you want to contribute anything?"

"You see, Mom," Jenny explains, "the only thing you have to offer another human being, ever, is your own state of consciousness. And how you do whatever it is you're doing, you're showing how evolved a human being you are."

Margaret laughs. "Oh, my goodness, Jenny, what is happening to my little girl!"

Jenny stands up and dances about the room with the mixing bowl in her arms. "My whole life," she declares, "is an exquisite dance, being in one role after another."

Margaret throws up her arms in mock exasperation. "Here, give me that!" she says to her daughter. Jenny hands her mother the bowl and they laugh together.

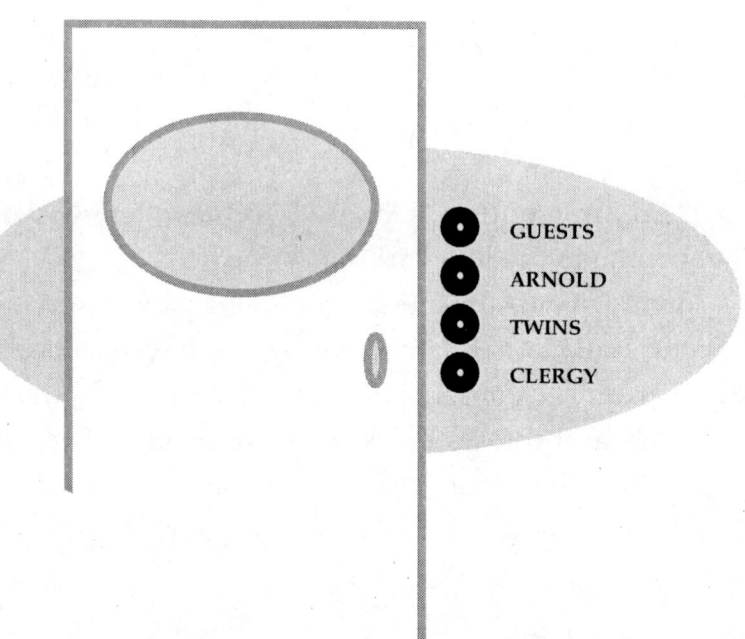

CHAPTER IX

The Priest and Jenny

The living room in the Spencer home is tasteful if not ostentatious with its decor in black and white. It's the grand piano that makes the black stand out, a striking contrast to the white sectional furniture and carpet. For tonight's special occasion, there is also a brilliant splash of crimson — pots of seasonal poinsettias aesthetically placed around the room.

It's the Spencer family annual sing-along Christmas Tea — and the guests will soon be arriving. Margaret inspects the dining room as a maid puts final touches on things. In the spirit of the event, she assures the bank manager's wife by singing.

Everything's ready, Miss Meggie
And everything's looking just fine
The waiter has polished the silver
And set out the glasses for wine

She points to the serving table.

The sandwiches, cookies and shortbread
And candies with ginger and lime
We will carry them in
When the cocktails begin
And we hope you have a really good time

A butler, hired for the occasion, along with a team of caterers shuffle into position. Priscilla and Angelina, both wearing tuxedos with white shirts and black bow ties, enter the room and take their positions beside the piano, on top of which sits a violin.

The doorbell chimes to its usual sound. "*Ding, ding, ding!*" The butler peers out the window and sings.

There goes the doorbell
Your guests, madam, they do arrive
I see neighbours and friends – and a lawyer!
Good heavens, I hope we survive!

He opens the door and ushers in the guests, including Samuel and Loretta Pebblebaum. The butler takes their coats, scarves and hats, all the time serenading them in the Spencer Christmas Tea tradition.

Gentlemen, greetings, and ladies
Why, Pebblebaum, you're looking prime

THE EUCHARIST

Won't you come on in
We're about to begin
And we hope you have a really good time

Caterers start to bustle about, carrying trays of fancy *hors d'oeuvres*. Wilbur makes a grand entrance, wearing a black suit with bright red necktie. He stands beside his wife Margaret, and with wine glasses in hand, they greet the guests in the Spencer tradition.

We welcome you all to our party
Delighted that you could be here
To share in the joys of the season
At our favourite time of the year
The waiters will serve you the hors d'oeuvres
The barmaid is pouring the wine
Try the salmon paté and the shrimp canapé
Raise a glass and drink to Auld Lang Syne

The guests, dressed in their finest, toast the event with a sip of wine and begin to savour the *hors d'oeuvres*.

The doorbell rings again, this time out of tune. "*Ding, ding, DONG!*" Priscilla and Angelina know the cue and dance toward the door.

That must be Arnold
He never could carry a tune

He wants to propose to our sister
And schedule a wedding in June
I don't think that she even likes him
And marriage is not on her mind

They open the door and greet the banking assistant. Arnold stands there, covered in snow, staring inside.

Arnold, come on in, we're about to begin
Remove your boots if you would be so kind

The doorbell rings once more, this time in double chimes. "Ding, ding! Ding, ding! Ding, ding!" The guests know the routine and quickly get into the act.

It's the spinsters!
Identical right from the start
They dressed like each other since childhood
Now no one can tell them apart
Neither of them ever married
Twin husbands aren't easy to find

The butler ushers in the twins as the guests serenade.

Won't you join in the fun
We've already begun
A celebration of the very best kind

THE EUCHARIST

Catherine and Dolores, as usual, are dressed alike and indistinguishable. They make their way across the room and sit down beside each other on the chesterfield.

Jenny enters, wearing a simple woolen dress with no make-up or jewelry. She looks around the room with obvious disapproval at the opulence. Margaret notices her daughter, leaves the guests at once and moves quickly to Jenny's side. "Jenny, dear," she whispers in a low voice, "do you have something a little more . . . ummm . . . a party dress, maybe."

"Oh, Mom!" says Jenny.

"For me, dear. Just this time," says Margaret.

Jenny sighs. "Okay . . . for you . . . just this time." She looks at Priscilla and Angelina standing beside the piano in their black tuxedos. "Why are they dressed like that?" she asks her mother.

"Oh, you know how your father always wanted a son," Margaret replies.

Jenny shakes her head.

"Run up now, dear, and change," her mother prods as she gives Jenny a quick kiss on the cheek. "And a little make-up and a necklace or something, okay?"

Jenny grimaces, shrugs her shoulders and leaves.

The doorbell rings again, this time to the deep sound of church bells. *"GONG! GONG! GONG!"*

The guests react in unison and burst into song.

Here come the clergy!
Good Lord! What are they doing here
Would somebody please hide the whisky
Would somebody else hide the beer

"Beer? There's beer?" asks Priscilla with excitement. Margaret and Wilbur stare at their daughter in shock.

Margaret goes to the door and greets Dean Potts and Michael, both in clerical garb. She ushers them in.

Why, Father, you look very charming
And the young man is simply sublime
Won't you come on through
The party's waiting for you
And we pray you'll have a really nice time

Priscilla notices Michael and glows. Angelina watches her sister and titters as Michael moves into the room and circulates freely among the guests. He is charming and the women quickly gravitate to him. Margaret pulls him away and takes him to where Catherine and Dolores are sitting.

"Aunties, I want you to meet Father Anthony," says Margaret.

Michael looks at the twins. "Hello. I'm Michael. And your names are?"

THE EUCHARIST

"Spencer," says Catherine.

"Spencer," repeats Dolores.

"And what are your Christian names?" Michael asks.

"Oh, Spencer is a good Christian name," responds Catherine.

"A good Christian name," repeats Dolores.

"Yes, I'm sure it is," Michael responds, "but what do people call you?"

"The Spencer sisters," answers Catherine.

"Spencer sisters," repeats Dolores.

"That's what they call you?" asks Michael.

Catherine laughs. "Or Spencer spinsters," she replies.

Dolores laughs in an identical fashion. "Or Spencer spinsters," she repeats.

"'Cause we're not married," adds Catherine.

"We're not married," repeats Dolores.

Michael is persistent. "I see," he says. "Now, when you were born, what names did your parents give you?"

"Catherine and Dolores," says Catherine.

"Catherine and Dolores," repeats Dolores.

"And does anyone call you Catherine and Dolores?" Michael wants to know.

"No," laughs Catherine, "because they can't tell us apart."

"Can't tell us apart," laughs Dolores.

"And who is who?" asks Michael.

Catherine, indicating with hand gestures, points first to herself, then to her sister. "Catherine and Dolores."

Dolores makes identical hand gestures. "Catherine and Dolores," she repeats.

Michael gives them both a warm smile. He looks at Catherine. "Well, it's a pleasure to meet you, Catherine." Then he looks at Dolores. "And a pleasure to meet you, Dolores."

The elderly twins raise their shoulders and titter. Just then Dean Potts steps in front of Michael and interrupts the conversation. "Michael, there you are."

"Dean Potts, you know Catherine and Dolores," Michael says.

"Yes. The Spencer sisters," replies the Dean. "How are we today, ladies?"

"We're fine," Catherine and Dolores reply in unison.

Dean Potts ushers Michael off to one side. Catherine and Dolores watch him leave, look at each other and titter again.

"Michael," says the Dean in a guarded voice, "better not talk about the Cathedral tonight. I'll explain later." He pats the priest on the shoulder and leaves.

Michael moves toward the piano where Priscilla is seated on the bench. Angelina stands beside her sister, holding a flute, as the two girls get ready to play their classical piece.

THE EUCHARIST

Margaret hushes the guests. "Ladies and gentlemen, can I have your attention for a moment, please. Every year on this occasion our daughters perform for you. This year Priscilla and Angelina are going to do a little melody for flute and piano."

The guests turn their attention to the two girls. Their conversation subsides as Priscilla and Angelina play their "Melody for Flute and Piano". When the number is done, the guests applaud appreciatively.

Michael walks over to the piano. "Very lovely," he says to the two girls. "Where did you learn to play like that?"

Priscilla beams and Angelina giggles. Michael picks up the violin. "Which one of you plays this?"

"Oh, we don't," says Priscilla. "It's our sister Jenny."

"She's home for Christmas . . . from college," offers Angelina.

"Oh, what's she studying?" Michael wants to know.

From across the room, Margaret beckons for Priscilla to come. Disappointed to be called away from Michael, she grudgingly leaves.

"Something impractical," replies Angelina.

Michael chuckles.

"Daddy thinks she should study Commerce but Mom says it wouldn't suit her 'cause she's hysteric," Angelina adds.

Michael gives her a puzzled look.

"And she's never gonna get married," Angelina adds.

"Well, in her case," replies Michael, "that's probably a good idea."

"Yeah, probably," says Angelina.

"Where is she now?" Michael asks.

"Oh, Mom sent her to her room."

Michael very carefully puts down the violin. Priscilla returns hurriedly and grins at the young priest dreamily.

"Well, I'll let you carry on," Michael says and leaves. Priscilla sighs with frustration.

Jenny descends the staircase and re-enters the room. She is now wearing a dress which is both modest and flattering, with appropriate jewelry and minimal make-up. We see how very beautiful she is. Jenny looks about, spots Catherine and Dolores at the far end of the living room and heads toward them. As she passes near the piano, Priscilla interrupts her.

"Mom wants us to do the 'Romance for Piano and Violin'," Priscilla informs her.

"Oh, no, I can't," Jenny replies. "I haven't played for a long time."

"She told me to tell you," Priscilla continues.

"Sorry," Jenny replies.

Jenny walks toward the twins. Arnold spots her and makes a beeline for her. He begins speaking before he gets close to her. "Jenny! Merry Chrithtmath!"

THE EUCHARIST

Jenny turns and sees him. She continues walking as she speaks. "Hello, Arnold. How are you?"

Arnold quickens his pace in an effort to catch up to her. "You're home for the holidayth."

"U-huh," Jenny answers, trying to avoid engaging in conversation. She maneuvers her way around the guests but a very determined Arnold stays in pursuit, dodging people in an attempt to keep up with her.

"Your father thaid you were coming," he continues.

"U-huh," Jenny replies. She gets nearer to Catherine and Dolores sitting on the chesterfield, moves in and sits down beside them. "Hello Aunties."

"Jenny, dear," says Catherine.

"Jenny, dear," echoes Dolores.

Arnold stands, hovering over them, staring at Jenny. "Tho . . . you like college?"

Jenny looks up. "Yes, Arnold, I do."

"Tho . . . what'th it like?"

"It's nice." Jenny tries to end the conversation but Arnold is persistent. "Like what thpethifically?"

"You want me to describe it in detail?" Jenny is a bit perturbed.

"That'd be thplendid," he replies.

Jenny grows exasperated. "When?"

"Are you bithy right now?" he asks.

Jenny looks around for an excuse. "Well, actually . . . I have to . . . play the violin right now." She excuses herself from the twins and abruptly heads for the piano.

While Jenny is finding a way out of her dilemma, Michael is engaged in conversation with her father, and there is a visible tension between them. Jenny gets to the piano, picks up her violin and starts to tune it. The shrill sound further strains her father's exchange with Michael.

"It's an old building, son," Wilbur says to Michael.

"May be so," Michael replies, "but it has beauty and character and history."

"It's falling down, son," Wilbur goes on.

"Needs some restoration, that's all," counters the young priest.

Wilbur is getting flushed. "It's seen its time, son," he insists.

Michael remains polite but one can see he is getting hot under the (clerical) collar. "Some things are timeless, sir," he replies. "And actually, it's not 'son'; it's 'Father'."

Wilbur realizes he has touched a nerve and decides not to push further. Michael composes himself as Jenny and Priscilla begin to play the very melodic "Romance for Piano and Violin". Michael turns his attention to the performance, using it as an excuse to end his unpleasant conversation with the bank manager. It is at this moment that he spots Jenny. He cannot take his eyes from her. In short, he is smitten! Wilbur notices Michael's instant infatuation and shudders.

As Jenny and Priscilla bring their violin and piano duet to a close, Margaret walks over and stands in the space between the two men. "Father, can I steal you," she says to Michael. "I'd like you to meet our oldest daughter Jenny."

Margaret takes his arm. Michael walks with her as if in a daze. "Jenny, this is Father Michael Anthony," says Margaret. "He's the new priest I was telling you about." Then she turns to Michael. "Jenny's home for Christmas. She's studying Philosophy."

Michael is lost for words. "Oh . . . how . . . practical. And your name is Jenny?"

"It's Jennifer," pipes up Angelina, "but we call her Jenny. Like I'm Angelina and they call me Angel. And my Mom's name is Margaret but Dad calls her Meg. And Priscilla—"

"Don't tell me, let me guess," interrupts Michael, trying to take part in the conversation. "It's . . . Prissy . . . No, it's . . . Silly . . . ohhhh . . ." He realizes his blunder and lowers his head in embarrassment. Priscilla could die on the spot!

"No," says Angelina laughing, "Priscilla doesn't have a nickname."

"Doesn't have a nickname," Michael repeats in despair as he puts his hands to his forehead. He tries to gain composure by changing the subject. He points to the tuxedos Priscilla and Angelina are wearing. "So . . . these are pretty classy outfits." He looks around the room decorated in simple but elegant black and white. "Seems that everything in this family is . . . black and white!" he adds as he laughs nervously.

Jenny points to his black and white clerical attire. Michael follows her hand movement and gets the clue. He throws his hands to his forehead again. "Ouch! Two in a row!"

Jenny looks at him expressionless, then tosses back her head and laughs.

The Spencer sing-along Christmas Tea comes to an end. Dean Potts and Michael exit the bank manager's home and amble down the street together. Michael is animated. The Dean is quiet.

"Great people. I like it here already," says the young priest.

"Michael, looks like there isn't going to be a role for you here after all," declares the Dean.

"What do you mean, sir?" Michael asks.

"Isn't gonna be a Cathedral," the Dean responds. "They're gonna tear it down."

Michael stops walking. "Who, sir?"

The Dean stops. "Some company called GEM . . . or G-E-M. They're putting up a development on the land."

THE EUCHARIST

"They can't do that!" declares Michael. "Can they?"

Dean Potts nods. "They can . . . and they are."

"But it's church property," Michael protests.

Dean Potts starts walking again. Michael follows. "The building . . . not the land," the Dean replies. "It's a lease . . . good only so long as the church shall stand. And the church is falling down."

Michael is adamant. "I cannot believe God has sent me here to witness the destruction of His church."

"God plays a mean game of chess sometimes," the Dean quips.

"Only to teach us to move wisely," Michael replies without hesitation.

Dean Potts is taken aback. "Pretty good! Learn that in seminary?"

"I learned that God doesn't act unless we act first," Michael replies.

"Well, things work a little different in this town, I'm afraid," says the Dean.

"God works the same everywhere," Michael replies.

Dean Potts does not respond. The two men continue walking in silence. Then the Dean speaks. "You'll do the pageant as planned."

"And after that?" Michael wants to know.

"I'll talk to the Archbishop about an alternative posting," says the Dean.

Michael stops walking. "I'm not leaving!"

Dean Potts stops walking and stares at him. "Priest playing chess with God?"

"No, sir," replies Michael with determination. "God playing chess with GEM."

Dean Potts throws his head back and laughs. "You're too much, you know that!"

"I'm in, win or lose," Michael says. "A deal?"

Dean Potts pauses. He tosses his head to one side and reflects. "Okay, it's a deal." They resume walking. "But no fancy moves, eh!" adds the Dean.

The two clergymen arrive at the Cathedral. Michael enters alone, looks around the sanctuary, then walks up to the altar, kneels at the communion rail and prays.

In this troubled world I come to you
You always seem to know just what to do
So now I kneel before your hallowed face
To still my mind and fill my soul with grace

I ask your guidance for another day
I ask your wisdom to know what to say
I ask your footprints so I'll find the way
Please hear me now

CHAPTER X

Michael and the Angel

The pageant rehearsal is about to take place inside the Cathedral. Michael, along with the Verger who is on hand to arrange the props, checks out the staging. Also present is Mrs. Pebblebaum, director of the children's choir, here to rehearse the pageant carol. Off to one side, children are trying on costumes of the holy family, the shepherds and wise men. Angelina quickly claims the angel costume.

"Okay, we're ready," says Michael. "Who wants to be Mary?" A little blond girl thrusts up her hand.

"Have to be a virgin!" shouts a smart-acting boy. The little blond girl shrugs, not understanding what this qualification means. The boys laugh.

"And we need a Joseph," says Michael. The boys point to Jason and push him toward the little blond girl. Jason reluctantly accepts the role.

"What's a virgin?" a second little boy wants to know.

"Person who looks after the church," offers a third.

"That's a verger, stupid," pipes up the smart-acting little boy. The boys play-fight and the girls titter as 'Mary' and 'Joseph' take their places.

"Jason's got a girlfriend," chides the smart-acting boy. Jason cowers with embarrassment.

Michael moves 'Mary' and 'Joseph' into position. "Okay, that's good. Can you get a little closer?" 'Mary' and 'Joseph' squeeze together reluctantly.

"Whew! Atta go, Jason!" shouts the smart-acting boy. Jason cowers.

"Never mind him," says Michael as he steps back and moves off to the side. "Okay, be ready to come in, shepherds. And . . . " he turns to Mrs. Pebblebaum, "start the music."

Mrs. Pebblebaum jumps up and swings into action. The children's choir begins to sing.

Shepherds in the field abiding
Watching o'er their flock by night
Angel voices bring glad tiding
And the heavens fill with light

The 'shepherds' are fooling around and miss their cue. "Shepherds!" shouts Michael, trying to get their attention as the choir starts singing the chorus.

Hal-le-lu-jah, ha-al-le-lu-u-jah

THE EUCHARIST

The shepherds march in, much too late! The chorus finishes.

Hal-le-lu-jah, ha-al-le-lu-u-jah

"Okay, wise men," instructs Michael, "you'll walk in from the other side and stand here." The 'wise men' move as directed. "Second verse, Mrs. Pebblebaum," instructs Michael. Mrs. Pebblebaum swings into action again and the children sing.

Wise men journey to the mangers
Bearing gifts of gold and myrrh
Mother Mary greets the strangers
Baby Jesus does not stir

Hal-le-lu-jah, ha-al-le-lu-u-jah
Hal-le-lu-jah, ha-al-le-lu-u-jah

"Very good!" exclaims Michael. "Now, where's our angel?"

Angelina, dressed in the angel costume, thrusts up her hand. Michael beckons her to come forward and points upward to a net. "Afraid of heights?" he asks.

Angelina reacts with fright.

"Don't worry," says Michael, "it'll hold you." He lifts Angelina to the suspended net. The Verger pulls a rope to hoist the net upward and fixes it into position.

Michael looks up at her. "Okay, angel, spread your wings." Angelina spreads her arms.

"And the lighting," Michael instructs.

The Verger turns a switch and "the heavens fill with light". The pageant performers rush from their positions to take a look.

"Ah, pretty!" shout the girls.

"Whew!" exclaim the boys.

Michael turns to Mrs. Pebblebaum. "Can we just try that hallelujah part now to see how it's all going to fit together." He beckons the children to resume their stage roles.

The pageant players shuffle back into position as Mrs. Pebblebaum swings into action. "Choir! Beginning of the chorus. Ready," she instructs.

The children's choir sings.

Hal-le-lu-jah, ha-al-le-lu-u-jah
Hal-le-lu-jah, ha-al-le-lu-u-jah

Everyone cheers and claps. "That's great!" says Michael. "And that's enough for today. We'll add the readings next time. Thanks, everyone."

THE EUCHARIST

The pageant players throw off their costumes and make for the door. The children in the choir disperse. The Verger turns off the lighting effects.

"It's going to be very nice," the Verger tells Michael.

"You think so?"

The Verger nods. "You would have done well here," he says to the young priest.

"I *will* do well here," Michael replies.

The Verger shakes his head and smiles as he leaves the sanctuary. Michael walks down the aisle toward the main door to exit. From above the staging platform, he hears a voice.

"How do I get down?"

Michael stops short. "Oh, my goodness!" he exclaims and returns to the stage. He looks up at Angelina and says jokingly, "What's an angel doing in my Cathedral?"

"What's a cathedral doing on my land?" Angelina rejoins without hesitation.

"Hark! The angel speaks!" says Michael, playfully. "Does it bring a message from heaven?" He unties the rope and helps Angelina down.

"No," she replies, "but I think my sister's in love with you."

"Do you, now. And what makes you think that?" he asks.

Angelina takes off her wings and hands them to Michael. "Because she keeps talking and talking about you. Daddy said, 'Good Lord, girl, can't you get that Anthony Michael off your brain!' He always says your name backwards."

Michael folds the angel wings. "He does, does he! And how long is your sister going to be home?"

"She's home all the time," Angelina replies.

"I thought she was just home for Christmas," says Michael.

"Oh, you mean Jenny," she replies.

Michael realizes his confusion but says nothing as Angelina leaves by the side door. After she has gone, Michael stands in the sanctuary of the Cathedral and ponders her words. "What's a cathedral doing on my land!" he repeats to himself. "Hmmm..."

CHAPTER XI

Michael and the Twins

There is a kinetic window display in the Spencer Department Store window. It alternates between Santa's Workshop and the Nativity. When the display shows Santa's workshop, the song goes like this . . .

Santa's loading up his sleigh
Elves are working every day
Listen close to what they say
In ecclesia Deo

And when the display shifts to the Nativity, the words change to . . .

Humble manger for a king
Shepherds watch and angels sing
Hear the tidings that they bring
In ecclesia Deo

Catherine and Dolores peer into the window and watch the display shift back and forth between the two scenes. Michael comes by and sees them. "Hi, there!" he says to them.

Catherine and Dolores turn around.

Michael looks at them. "Let me guess." He points to Catherine. "You're Catherine," he says. Then he points to Dolores. "And you're Dolores." He gives them a warm smile.

"It's a miracle!" says Catherine.

"A miracle!" echoes Dolores.

Michael laughs. "You think so?"

"Yes, 'cause no one can tell us apart!" explains Catherine.

"No one can tell us apart!" repeats Dolores.

"You know, that's something I'm a little curious about," Michael says. "You look alike, you dress alike, you even talk alike. But your names are very different."

"Well, I was named after our aunt," offers Catherine.

"She was named after our aunt," repeats Dolores.

"She died very young," says Catherine.

"Very young," echoes Dolores.

"Oh, that's sad," says Michael. "What happened to her?"

"No one knows," says Catherine.

"No one knows," repeats Dolores.

"Such a dear thing she was," says Catherine.

"Dear thing she was," echoes Dolores.

THE EUCHARIST

"Yes, I'm sure," says Michael. He looks at Dolores. "And who were you named after?"

Catherine answers for her. "No one."

Dolores repeats the response. "No one."

"No one?" Michael questions. "Well, maybe you were named after Mary, the mother of Jesus."

"Oh, for heaven's sake!" says Catherine.

"Heaven's sake!" repeats Dolores.

"Well, that's what your name means," Michael tells her. "Did you know that?"

"Didn't know that!" states Catherine.

"Didn't know that!" repeats Dolores.

Michael continues. "Yes. 'Dolores'. It comes from 'Mater Dolorosa'. It means 'Mother of Sorrow'."

"But she's not even a mother!" exclaims Catherine.

"Not even a mother!" repeats Dolores.

"Well, that's what your name means," he says.

"Imagine that!" says Catherine.

"Imagine that!" says Dolores.

"Well, I must be off," Michael tells them. "You ladies enjoy your outing."

"Oh, yes, we will," titters Catherine.

"Yes, we will," titters Dolores.

Michael starts to leave. Catherine calls out to him. "Wait a minute. What does 'Catherine' mean?"

Dolores repeats the question. "What does 'Catherine' mean?"

Michael stops. "'Catherine'. . . hmmm," he ponders. "You know something, I don't know . . . but I'll find out." He points to Catherine. "That's a promise!" He smiles at the twins and walks away.

Catherine points at Dolores and mimics Michael. "That's a promise!" she giggles.

Dolores points at Catherine and repeats the gesture. "A promise!" she giggles.

The twins take each other's hands and titter together.

CHAPTER XII

And They Called Him Emmanuel

Michael searches through church records inside the Cathedral office. The Verger walks by the doorway. "Got a minute?" Michael calls out to him.

"What can I do for you?" the Verger replies.

"Know anything about the history of this place?" asks Michael.

"How do you mean?"

"Well, it says here the land belongs to the Cathedral 'so long as the church shall stand'. If the building were not here, whose land would this be?"

"Wilbur Spencer's," the Verger replies.

"How come?" Michael wants to know.

"His great grandfather, the one who built the church, he had two sons," explains the Verger. "The old man left one son all his land and the other all his money. The son who got the land was Wilbur's grandfather, and it was passed on down to him. The twins, Wilbur's aunts, they got all the money."

"What about the old man's daughter, Catherine?" Michael asks.

"Oh, she died very young," the Verger explains.

"What happened to her?" asks Michael.

"Don't know," replies the Verger. "Nobody seems to know. Except that she went away. And then she died. They never talked about it."

"Did you know the old man?" asks Michael.

"Can't say that I did," the Verger replies, "but I've always felt it was because of him that I'm here."

"Really?" says Michael.

"Yes," the Verger replies. "I grew up in a home, you know. The day I turned fourteen, the old man came there and said I had this job, and that it was mine 'as long as the church shall stand'. Of course, I figured it would stand a lot longer than I would."

The young priest grows pensive. "Where were you christened?" he asks.

"Oh, I wasn't christened," says the Verger.

"Not christened? What name did you go by?"

"At the home they called me Emmanuel," the Verger replies.

"Emmanuel. That means 'God with us'. Did you know that?" asks Michael.

"They never said what it meant," replies the Verger. "And after that they just called me Verger."

THE EUCHARIST

There is silence for a moment. Then Michael becomes animated. "You've been here all your life," he says to the Verger. "They can't do this!"

"It's what they call progress," the Verger responds.

"They're just closing the door on it," protests Michael vehemently.

"Well, the way I see it," the Verger replies, "a door is never closed meaninglessly. Something twice as good will come of this. Just wait and see."

"How can you be so . . . calm about it?" Michael asks.

"Just a feeling I have," he replies. "Can't explain it."

"Well, if you figure it out," says Michael, "please let me know."

Support the
G E M
Telethon
Christmas Eve

CHAPTER XIII

The Priest and Jenny Again

Jenny saunters down Main Street toward Cathedral Square. Michael is outside the church, putting up a big banner alongside the "Save the Cathedral" sign. It reads: "Support the G E M Telethon Christmas Eve". The letters G, E and M are big and bold.

Jenny approaches and sees him. "Hello!" she says.

Michael stops, turns to see her and breaks out in an awkward grin. "Why, hello there!" he says. He points to the parcels she is carrying. "Christmas shopping?"

"Oh, a little bit," she replies. "What's this all about?"

"Just what it says," he responds. "We need to raise some money for the Cathedral. They want to—"

"You're gonna raise money on Christmas Eve?" she questions.

"Yeah, it's urgent. Somebody wants to—"

He doesn't get a chance to finish. "What does G E M stand for?" she asks him.

"Gold, Encense and Myrrh," he replies, "the name of the pageant."

"Incense starts with an 'I', not an 'E'," she points out.

"Yeah, I know," he says, "but I put it that way for a reason."

"Well, why don't you just put the whole title up there? Nobody will know what it means."

"Oh, they'll know," says Michael.

"How?" Jenny asks.

"It's all part of the plan," Michael replies.

"Ohhh . . . sounds cunning," she says.

"More like confronting, I'd say."

"Well, the problem with confrontation," states Jenny, "is that no matter what the short-term goal, there is long term loss."

"Yeah, well," Michael retorts, "without this short-term goal, the long-term loss will be the Cathedral."

Jenny crosses her arms with parcels hanging in front. "So this is what they brought you here to do, is it?"

"No, actually, it's something I decided to do on my own."

"Solicit money for a building?" she questions.

"Yeah, I guess you could say that."

"Well, good luck." She takes a few steps to leave.

Michael tries to detain her. "Hey, listen, would you like to help?"

"Sorry, not my thing."

"What do you mean?"

"I don't want to come to the aid of a building."

THE EUCHARIST

Michael is taken aback. "Oh, you don't! What do you want to come to the aid of, then?"

"People who are suffering," she replies.

Michael is getting slightly irritated. "Oh, really! And without the Cathedral, how do you propose we find them?"

"Go where they are," Jenny answers assuredly.

"Oh, I see, and where is that?" Michael is frustrated.

"I don't know . . . wherever there is suffering. Like where there's poverty . . . or a drought . . . or maybe an earthquake. There are lots of places."

Michael is thoroughly triggered now. "You've got it all figured out, haven't you!"

"Not really, but I see the Cathedral as other than a building."

"Well, seeing the Cathedral as other is the problem."

Jenny corrects him. "Seeing another human being as other is the problem."

"Well, in this case, the problem is another human being."

"You speak in tongues instead of parables," Jenny chides.

Michael is angry now. "You think God wants me to stand by and watch His Cathedral fall to the ground?"

"Oh, I think he knows how it is," Jenny responds as she walks away.

"Oh, do you now? And how is it?" Michael calls after her.

Jenny shouts back. "Better ask him. He's the one who's writing the script."

"Oh, really!" he shouts back. He stands motionless with his hands on his hips. "Thank God she's never getting married!" he mumbles to himself.

CHAPTER XIV

Michael and the Vision

Michael enters the Cathedral. He is in an extremely agitated state, mumbling to himself as though reliving his frustrating conversation with Jenny. In spite of his resistance to her comments, she seems to have created in him a serious doubt. He walks behind the communion rail and looks back at the sanctuary. He is troubled. So he does what he does whenever he is troubled: he prays.

> *Is the soul reborn inside a worn cathedral*
> *Is a stained glass window the writing on the wall*
> *Do I meditate to recreate a miracle*
> *'Cause that's not where the action is at all*
>
> *So tell me, Jesus, where your people can find you*
> *And tell me, Jesus, what your people can do*
> *'Cause they're crying on the mountain*
> *from the earthquake pain*
> *And they're dying on the desert*
> *where the sky won't rain*
> *I need a little inspiration again from you*

It is time for the Eucharist. Worshippers arrive and settle into the pews. Dean Potts enters, dressed in his clerical attire, and takes his place at the altar. He prepares the sacraments. The faithful step forward to receive the bread and wine. Michael, oblivious to what is going on around him, stares motionless at the scene. His thoughts are racing.

> *The sacred frills can send the thrills right through ya*
> *But it's hard to find You in that wine and bread*
> *And while I'm singing to Ya a heartfelt hallelujah*
> *My mind is on the people left unfed*

He shifts his gaze from the altar and stares up at the stained glass window of the mother and child.

> *Where are you, where are you, Jesus*
> *Am I getting through, getting through to you, Jesus*
> *I said they're crying on the . . .*

And now something supernatural seems to happen. A single beam of light streams in through the stained-glass window. It expands, filling the sanctuary. Michael looks back at the communicants attending the Eucharist. They appear now as he has never witnessed them before: they are a mass of poor and hungry people — and the communion line is a bread line.

THE EUCHARIST

Michael turns his attention back to the stained glass window. The Madonna-like mother and child is now a starving mother holding her dying child. Michael stares at the window, then back at the mass of suffering people. He shakes his head in disbelief.

As quickly as it appeared, the vision disappears, and Michael realizes he is at the celebration of the Eucharist. He stands there, behind the communion rail, watching as Dean Potts serves the remaining few at the end of the line. He gazes about, bewildered. He looks up again at the stained-glass window but it appears as it was before: the Madonna-like mother and child.

Michael wanders down the aisle in a confused state, and stands at the rear of the sanctuary. He turns and looks back on the scene, now questioning his very role as a priest in an established religious institution.

Is your spirit found upon a round new altar
Does it speak to man in prayer and litany
Or seek to find those left behind to falter
To bear their load and share their misery

The transformation is complete.

Now I hear, I hear you, Jesus
Loud and clear
You're getting near to me, Jesus

Oh, you're crying on the mountain
from the earthquake pain
And you're dying on the desert
where the sky won't rain
I found you there among the wretched again

The Eucharist is over. The congregation sings the closing hymn. Michael mouths the final words in time to the music . . .

Hallelu . . . hallelu . . . hallelujah

Nothing has ever been so clear to him. And nothing will ever be the same.

CHAPTER XV

Michael and the Dean Again

Dean Potts stands at the window in his church office, staring out. Michael stands beside the doorway inside the room. "I don't need to tell you, I suppose," begins the Dean.

"No, sir, . . . I realize . . . I was . . . negligent," Michael replies. "I just . . . well, I don't know what came over me."

"You were not paying attention!" states the Dean adamantly.

"I know. It was like I was . . ." Michael tries to explain but cannot.

Dean Potts walks over and looks straight at him. "Don't let it happen again, hear me?" he warns.

"Yes, sir," Michael replies.

"Okay, that's all," says the Dean.

"Yes, sir." Michael starts to leave, and then he stops. "Ummm . . . there is something. No, well, no, there isn't."

"What is it?" harps the Dean.

"Well, I don't know how to . . ." Michael is lost for words.

"Speak up," instructs the Dean, impatiently.

"Well, about this tearing down of the Cathedral," Michael says.

"We've got two weeks," answers the Dean, curtly.

"Yes, but if the Cathedral goes, so does the land," says Michael.

"That's the deal," states the Dean.

"Wilbur Spencer. It would be his land, right?" asks Michael.

"It's Spencer land," the Dean confirms.

"Well, this GEM business," says Michael. "I mean, I wonder if there's something . . ."

"What're you getting at?"

"Well," Michael tries to explain, "G-E-M is M-E-G spelled backwards . . . and . . . no, no, it's nothing."

"We've got two weeks, Michael," repeats the Dean. "And Wilbur will do what he can. He keeps this church running."

"I'm sure he does," mumbles Michael, half under his breath.

CHAPTER XVI

The Mother and the Virgin

Michael stares into the window at the Spencer Department Store, watching the kinetic display alternate between Santa's Workshop and the Nativity.

Santa's loading up his sleigh
Elves are working every day
Listen close to what they say
In ecclesia Deo

Humble manger for a king
Shepherds watch and angels sing
Hear the tidings that they bring
In ecclesia Deo

Jenny walks up and starts to enter the Department Store. She sees Michael, stops and turns to him. "Like it?" she asks.

Michael is taken aback. "Well, hello there!"

"What do you think of it?"

"The window?" Michael says. "It's . . . ummm, yes, I like it . . . but there's a confusion between the sacred and the secular."

"You think so?"

"Yeah, don't you?"

"No," she says adamantly.

"Well, elves don't go about singing 'In ecclesia Deo'," he points out.

"And angels do?" Jenny asks.

"Well . . . yeah," he mumbles.

"How do you know?"

"It just doesn't fit, that's all."

Jenny looks straight at him. "I designed it."

Michael is taken aback again. "You did?"

"Yeah, a couple of years ago. Daddy couldn't decide between Santa's Workshop and the Nativity. I said why not both. Then maybe people would get the connection between the two."

"How do you mean?" Michael asks.

"Well, people make artificial distinctions," she replies. "Like in the Eucharist, they think communion bread is sacred but other bread isn't. To me, the idea of having sacred bread in communion is to remind us that all bread is sacred."

"That's . . . well . . . it's a different interpretation," he replies. "Don't know where it would lead."

"Well, it would lead to feeding the hungry, wouldn't it?" she says.

"You have a really unusual way of seeing things," says Michael.

"It's quite simple," she explains. "People think things are different when they're actually identical."

"Well, maybe, but . . ." He stops short. "Identical! Do you know what 'Catherine' means?" he asks her.

"Catherine who?"

"No, the name 'Catherine'," he says. "What does it mean?"

"It means 'pure'," Jenny replies.

"Pure?" Michael is motionless.

"Yes, pure. You know, like the Virgin Mary."

Michael stares at her. Then he becomes very excited. "The pure virgin . . . the mother of sorrow . . . it's the same person!"

Jenny is astonished at his naiveté. "Yeah," she says.

Michael grows ecstatic. "The same person. She had a son . . . Emmanuel . . . ohhhhh!"

Jenny looks at him with disbelief. "You didn't know that?"

"I just figured it out!" he says. "Oh, my goodness!"

"Michael, you're a priest!" she says. "Where have you been!"

Michael is too excited to respond. "It's a miracle!" he says. "I've got to tell the Verger!"

Jenny laughs. "He doesn't know it either?"

"Oh, Jenny," he exclaims, "I can't tell you what this means!"

"Good Lord, Michael," she responds. "I learned it in Sunday School!"

"I've got to go!" he utters hurriedly. "Oh, the Verger will be ecstatic!" He runs off.

"Maybe you should tell the Dean too!" Jenny shouts after him as he rushes down the street. She puts her hand on her forehead. "Good gracious!" she mutters to herself as she enters the Spencer Department Store.

CHAPTER XVII

The Sermon on the Mount

Michael is conducting a program with a group of youngsters in the church basement. Banners on the wall read "Kids Can!" and "It's Up to YOUth". He hands out song sheets and instructs the youngsters in the playing of the pop instruments.

The four delinquents are among the youths, beating away on the drums. The reverberation is loud. Dean Potts sits at his desk in his upstairs office, cupping his hands over his ears in annoyance to the rock music.

Gentle Jesus, meek and mild
I know you're not the only child
Who grew up with a vision
Of just what the world could be
For your message comes out loud and strong
Above the hum of choir song
It's in the air, it's everywhere
It calls to you and me

Angelina rushes in, pulling Jenny by the hand and pointing to the guitars and drums. "You gotta hear this!" she says excitedly to her oldest sister, then runs over and joins the group.

Michael notices Jenny standing there alone. He looks expectantly at her. "Okay if I listen?" she silently mouths to him, gesturing.

Michael nods approval and turns back to the group. Jenny sits down nearby. She marvels at the words the young people are singing.

> *If you want to change the world somehow*
> *People, come together now*
> *Come and bring about the world you'd like to see*
> *If you care about the human race*
> *Come on now and take your place*
> *Come and rid the world of things that should not be*

The drums are beating and the guitars are twanging. The four delinquent boys are having a great time. Jenny smiles with delight and nods her approval. But poor Dean Potts, trying to concentrate on his work upstairs, can take no more. He gets up from his desk and struts down to the basement as the young people sing on.

> *Make peace with your brother*
> *Love those who show you scorn*

THE EUCHARIST

Give food to those who hunger
And comfort those who mourn

The Dean pokes his head into the room and watches from the sideline. The youths complete the song.

Forgive the one who wrongs you
Always walk that second mile
Give what you can when
  you are asked to share
And make your brother's burden
  less to bear

Jenny stands up and claps vigorously. Michael looks in her direction and smiles. Dean Potts makes a coughing sound to get Michael's attention, and then beckons him to come over to the side of the room.

"What is this?" asks the Dean in an agitated state.

"The Sermon on the Mount," Michael replies.

"That's the Sermon on the Mount?" shouts the Dean.

"It's the way they get it," Michael tries to explain. "They don't respond to the ritual of the—"

"That's your job, Michael," the Dean interrupts, "to get them to respond. We're a church, not a rock 'n' roll club."

Michael protests. "But this is what you brought me here to do. To revitalize the church by attracting young people. Look at them. Even those young boys who were pelting snowballs at the—"

The Dean interrupts him again. "Let's talk about this upstairs, shall we." He shouts to the youths. "Okay, kids, party's over. Time to go."

The youngsters look at the Dean, then to Michael. Michael gestures for them to obey. Reluctantly, they pick up their coats and saunter out of the building.

Jenny stands there, watching it all unfold. She looks at Michael. He shrugs as he follows the Dean to the church office.

CHAPTER XVIII

It's All About Miracles

Jenny leaves the Cathedral and stands off to the side of the building. She watches as the youngsters, led by the delinquent boys, aim snowballs at the bell on top of the wall. None can hit it. A few minutes later, Dean Potts emerges and catches sight of the youths. "Hey, quit that! Before you smash something!" he yells at them.

The youngsters stop and look at him. The Dean waves a dismissing hand at them. "Go home now. It's suppertime," he shouts. The youngsters disperse. The Dean, not noticing Jenny, continues down the steps of the Cathedral, mumbling to himself. "Who puts kids up to these things!" He walks away.

Jenny saunters back up the Cathedral steps and waits outside the door. A few moments later, a very dejected Michael appears. Jenny smiles at him. "Wanna go for a walk?" she asks him tenderly.

"I need one," Michael replies.

"That's a great thing you're doing with those kids," she tells him.

"Or foolhardy," he replies. "It's not what they want here." They stroll into the park beside the Cathedral.

"I feel like I incited you or something," Jenny says to him with compassion.

Michael is despondent. "Oh, no . . . nothing like . . ." He looks at her and something in her demeanor makes him lighten up. His manner suddenly becomes playful. "Well, now," he retorts, "maybe you did! Yeah! You got a spell on me or something? Somebody put you up to this?"

Jenny laughs and jokes back. "Maybe."

"Well, it's workin'. Just came from the Dean's office."

"And?" Jenny probes.

"One more 'fancy move' and I'm out."

"Well, nothing happens by accident," she responds.

Michael stops walking and looks at her. "Where do you get all this?"

"Get what?"

"This . . . philosophy of life . . . or whatever you call it." Michael resumes walking.

Jenny shrugs. "From life, then, I guess."

"How can you be so . . . I don't know, so nonchalant about everything?" he says.

"Because everything is connected to everything else," she replies.

"You've got an answer for everything, haven't you!" Michael says. "Some of them pretty good answers too!"

THE EUCHARIST

"Well, the world does what it does," Jenny replies.

"See, there you go. There's another one," he says. "The world does what it does. How do you come up with those?" Michael pauses, then continues. "Yeah, well, the world is gonna knock down a Cathedral unless somebody comes up with a pretty quick miracle." He turns to her. "Don't suppose you've got any of those, have ya?"

"You want a miracle?" says Jenny.

"Yeah, I need a miracle," he says lightheartedly. "You handin' them out too?"

"There are miracles all around you, Michael," she replies.

"Oh, there are, are there!" he challenges. "Well, I don't see any! Maybe you can get one of them to stop going around and land right here in my hand." He looks directly at her. "Can you do that?"

Jenny giggles.

Michael becomes more enthusiastic, swinging his arms in the air. "Then, you see . . . I'll hang it on top the Cathedral and they'll come with their . . . jack hammers and their . . . wrecking machines and everything . . . and they won't be able to knock it down, see."

Jenny laughs.

Michael stops walking and faces her. "You got a miracle that'll do that?"

"It all depends on what you call a miracle," Jenny replies.

"Ah, there's the catch!" Michael starts walking again. "Yeah, I knew there would be a catch. Yeah . . ."

"I see lots of miracles," says Jenny.

"Okay, c'mon, show 'em to me anyway. Maybe I can make do with one of 'em."

You want a miracle?" Jenny says . . .

The stars and the planets
The comets, the granites
The rocks that give birth to the sand
You want a miracle
The prairies, the mountains
The meadows, the fountains
The seas that wash the land
It is the rainbow that plays in the light
The shadow that stays in the night
Life is all about miracles
Right in the palm of your hand

"Ah, I gotcha!" Michael exclaims. "Two can play this game, you know!" He stretches out his arms and creates his own bit of poetry.

You want a miracle
The grasses, the heather

THE EUCHARIST

The blossoms, the weather
The seeds that give birth to the grain
You want a miracle
The daylight, the hours
The seasons, the flowers
The clouds that turn to rain
It is the morning call of the loon
The evening lull of the moon
Life is all about miracles
Sung to a cosmic refrain

Jenny claps her hands and they laugh together. Michael reaches out and takes Jenny's hand. She responds. In more than one way, they start making poetry together, line by line . . .

You want a miracle
The air and the waters
The trees and the otters
The whales that give birth in the sea
You want a miracle
The fathers, the mothers
The sisters, the brothers
Their love for you and me
It is the streams that flow in the wild
The dreams that grow in a child
Life is all about . . .

They cannot finish the verse. They stop walking and look into each other's eyes. Then Michael reaches out and pulls Jenny to him passionately.

"Oh, Jenny!" Michael cries, holding her tightly.

Jenny stands motionless. Then she extends her arms around his waist and returns the hug with a mixture of passion and confusion.

CHAPTER XIX

Gold, Ensense and Myrrh

Christmas Eve! The sanctuary of the Cathedral has been transformed into a theatre for the GEM telethon. The space behind the communion rail—right beneath the prominent stained-glass window—is the stage on which the Nativity pageant will be performed.

The townsfolk have turned out in full force, and the pews are filled to overflowing. The local television station is on hand to bring live coverage of the fund-raising event. Their mobile unit is parked outside, while inside, lighting and sound technicians make final touches as two cameramen take up their positions. The Floor Director, wearing a mouthpiece and earphones, stands off to one side while the Commentator, microphone in hand, takes his position in front of one camera. A row of telephone volunteers, poised to record the pledges, is seated in the front pew.

The event begins with a Processional. From the back of the sanctuary, altar boys appear, carrying a cross and lighted candles. Dean Potts and Father Michael Anthony walk behind them, followed by the pageant players and the children's choir, singing the new Christmas carol.

> *Jesus was a little child*
> *Born into a manger*
> *There he lay so meek and mild*
> *To the world a stranger*
>
> *Shepherds keeping watch at night*
> *In the fields abiding*
> *Saw the heavens fill with light*
> *Heard the angel tiding*
>
> *Wise men journey from afar*
> *Precious gifts they carry*
> *Guided by a wondrous star*
> *To the mother Mary*

They take their appropriate positions at the front of the Cathedral. The altar boys light the candles on the altar as the children's choir completes the carol.

> *Peace on earth from God above*
> *Hear the angel voices*
> *Jesus is the Lord of love*
> *All the world rejoices*

THE EUCHARIST

Christ the king was born for us
Lift your voice in singing
Hallelujah, glorious
Christmas bells are ringing

When the music ends, Michael makes his way to the pulpit. He speaks directly to the gathered audience. "On this Christmas Eve," he begins, "we come together for a very special reason. As you well know, the Cathedral is threatened by the forces of change. If we are to save the church, we must act. We have invited the cameras along so people outside these walls can see what we are doing here. And all these volunteers, staffing the telephones, they are here to take people's calls. Now, when we get a signal from the Floor Director here, the performance will begin. So just sit back and . . ."

The Floor Director gives the signal.

"Ah, I think we are ready now," Michael says. He steps from the pulpit.

The lights go down. The candles on the altar pierce the darkness. One can hear the pageant players shuffling into position. The four delinquent boys also take their places.

The television lights come up on the Commentator. "Good evening, ladies and gentlemen, boys and girls," he begins, "and welcome. We are coming to you live from the Mother of Sorrow Cathedral for this special

Christmas Eve telethon. The performance tonight is called G-E-M . . . which stands for 'Gold, Encense and Myrrh' and . . . you know, this is just an aside, but I always thought incense was spelled with an 'i' . . . Well, as I was saying, with the help of all you good people out there in Televisionland, as well as the audience right here in the Cathedral, we hope to raise enough money to save this great building. So stay with us and settle back now as we bring you a very special musical performance."

The lights come up on the staging. One can now see the pageant players in their traditional roles. But the similarity stops there. The scene is not Bethlehem; it is a drought-stricken desert. 'Mary' with the infant Jesus is a mother holding a dying child. 'Joseph', the shepherds and wise men are similarly destitute. All of the pageant players are draped in clothing that is torn and worn, coloured in a dingy grey.

The delinquent boys, singing as a quartet, perform the verses of a song while the pageant players act out the story being told in the lyrics.

> *She wrapped her garment round her frame*
> *To shield it from the sun*
> *She stood in line upon the cracking sand*
> *Her children crouched beside her*
> *The two that still survived*
> *The victims of a dry unyielding land*

THE EUCHARIST

She had known the pain of poverty
The threat of tribal war
Survival held an element of fear
She understood the hardship of nomadic desert life
But never had the drought been so severe

The children's choir sings the chorus.

Mother of sorrow
Your eyes too weak for crying
You stare into the camera
Now the world can watch you dying

The quartet follows with a second verse.

She thought about the weeks they walked
The days they stood in line
About her child that died along the way
There was no time for sorrow then
She left it by the road
A second child would surely die today
The rations were distributed
The woman took their share
She held her dying child and tried to cry
She took the rations for the three
And fed them to the one
The strongest child could live if they could die

Once again, the children sing the chorus. Then the quartet proceeds with the final verse.

> *Officials move along the line*
> *To segregate the strong*
> *Rations were for those who might abide*
> *The woman kissed her strongest child*
> *And left it in the line*
> *Then held her dying child and stepped aside*
> *The camera scanned the starving mob*
> *It rested on her frame*
> *She saw her still reflection in the lens*
> *She heard the commentator say*
> *The child was not alive*
> *And this is how the story often ends*

The children's choir concludes the pageant performance by singing the chorus one last time.

> *Mother of sorrow*
> *Your eyes too weak for crying*
> *You stare into the camera*
> *Now the world can watch you dying*

The pageant completed, the players leave the stage. The lights go down, then come up on the Commentator.

THE EUCHARIST

There is a lingering silence. Nothing stirs . . . not even a television Commentator! He stands bewildered, under the glare of the television lights, not knowing what to say or do. But the show must go on!

"Ah . . . ladies and gentlemen . . . " the Commentator begins, "that . . . ah . . . " He is clearly lost for words. He turns to the Floor Director. "Is the phone number going up on the screen now? Or is . . . what's the . . ."

The Floor Director shrugs. He looks to the Dean for direction. Dean Potts is in shock.

"Ladies and gentlemen," the Commentator begins again, "this is a bit different from the program we . . . If you want to make a . . . " He turns to the Dean. "Do they make a pledge now? Do you want to say something about this?"

Dean Potts, in a confused state, wanders over to the microphone.

"We're going to talk now with the Dean of the Cathedral," the Commentator announces. "Dean Potts, can you tell us about the program here tonight."

"Yes, well, actually . . . it's . . . ah . . ." stumbles the Dean. "You know, we're presenting this program to . . . raise money for the repair of the Cathedral . . ."

"This is a rather . . . ah . . . different interpretation of the Christmas story," interjects the Commentator. "How does it fit in with the idea of raising money to repair the building?"

"Well . . . I guess it would be the idea that . . . ah . . . " Dean Potts is floundering badly. He looks about for Michael and sees him standing off to the side. "Maybe Father Anthony over there could speak to that. Ah . . . he's the one responsible for the . . . ah . . . program here tonight." He beckons to Michael. "Father Anthony, do you want to step over here?"

Dean Potts moves hastily out of the spotlight, brushing by Michael as they switch places. "You'd better have a good explanation for this!" he whispers to the young priest.

Michael takes his position beside the Commentator.

"That was a very ah . . . moving presentation," states the Commentator.

"Did that move you?" states Michael. "Well, good. It moved me too. Something needs to move us. Because somebody wants to move you and me and everybody else right out of here. They want to knock this Cathedral to the ground so they can put up a development and pull the gold and everything else right out of our pockets. Well, let them do it, I say. Let them tear down this creaky old building. Who needs it!"

"But isn't the whole idea to save the building?" asks the Commentator. "Isn't that what we're—"

"A Cathedral is not a building, for goodness sake," Michael interrupts. "It's not bricks and stone and . . . those uncomfortable wooden pews. It's not that fancy pulpit or . . . that stained glass window. Heavens no, the Cathedral is not a building. The Cathedral is people."

There is silence. The Commentator shrugs and looks at the Floor Director who indicates for him to carry on.

"But the purpose of the telethon here tonight, as I understand it," continues the Commentator, "is to—"

Michael interrupts once again. "The point I'm trying to make is that we're not in the business of saving buildings. No, we're in the business of saving people."

The Commentator struggles to remain composed.

Michael turns to the congregation. "So I ask you, do you want to support the movement of a building . . . or the building of a movement?"

Dean Potts throws his head back in disbelief.

Michael carries on. "See those offering plates sitting there on the altar. Well, come on up here and stuff your money in them if you want to prop up this musty old building. But I'm not going to ask you to do that." He looks directly into the camera. "And I'm not going to ask you people out there to do it either. Never mind the building. Jesus didn't need a building. No, he went about feeding the hungry, healing the sick. That's what we're supposed to be doing."

The Commentator looks to the Dean. The Dean is in distress. He then looks to the Floor Director. The Floor Director shrugs.

Michael is on a roll! "Well, maybe I don't know what I'm saying. But I do know this. The church should be giving money to people instead of taking it from them. That's what we're here for . . . to give, not to take. So if you want to help people who need it . . . or if you need help yourself, call us. The phones are there. They'll put the number up on the screen."

The Floor Director speaks into his headgear, and the phone number appears on the screen. Dean Potts puts his head in his hands.

Michael carries on. "Just call that number. And we'll do what we can to help. That's what we're here for. If you don't have enough food this Christmas . . . if you lost your job or you're sick or something . . . Maybe you're by yourself for the holidays and you're lonely. Because, you know, there's more than one kind of hunger . . ."

Dean Potts gestures the "cut" signal to the young priest to get him to stop. Michael gets the message. "Well, that's all I've got to say," he adds. "And have a merry Christmas. Because that's what it's all about. Being happy and having enough to eat and helping each other and . . . things like that . . . So phone us if you want to be part of this and, while you're doing that, these kids here are going to sing for you."

Michael starts to leave. The Commentator stands motionless. Then Michael takes the microphone. "And one more thing," he says, "this song they're doing, these four young boys, they wrote it themselves. They're a good bunch of kids." He hands the microphone back to the Commentator. Then he leans back to make one more comment. "And it's a darn good song, too."

Michael steps aside. The phones start ringing as the quartet sings.

If we really knew
How very little it would take
If we really knew
How easy it would be to make
A world that works for everyone
A family of man
Everybody can

The phones are now ringing "off the hook". The confused volunteers take messages while looking about for direction.

If we really knew
That hunger does not need to be
If we really knew
It all depends on you and me
A planet whirling round the sun
Where everybody shares
Everybody cares

The phones keep ringing. The volunteers struggle to keep up, taking calls as quickly as they can.

Gold and frankincense and mirth
Lift your voices high
So every child upon the earth
Can live to see the sky

The music ends—but the phones keep right on ringing. Not knowing what else to do, the Floor Director gives the signal to cut the television lights.

The lights fade. The Commentator puts down his microphone and wipes the sweat from his forehead.

Dean Potts marches over to where the young priest is standing. "You're fired!" he states angrily.

"No, I'm not," Michael replies calmly, "I quit!"

CHAPTER XX

Wilbur and the Enterprise

Christmas day comes and goes. Inside the Spencer living room, Margaret tidies up as Wilbur mulls over some papers. Jenny, who did not attend the Christmas Eve telethon and wants no knowledge of it, is ironing in an adjoining room, listening to the radio. The door between the rooms is partially open.

"What are you working on, dear?" Margaret asks her husband.

"Oh, some plans for a meeting," Wilbur replies. He cannot hide his exuberance. "This town's gonna have a spanking new shopping mall!"

"How exciting," Margaret responds. "Where are you going to put it?"

"Oh, there alongside the Department Store," replies Wilbur. "Well, the store will be part of the mall. Oh, that reminds me, the window display isn't working. Can you ask Jenny to stop by and fix it. She's the only one who seems to know how to do it."

"Won't the space be a little crowded, dear?" she asks.

"Oh, no. Plenty of room for her to maneuver."

"No dear, not the window. The mall. There's not enough space for a shopping mall, is there?"

"Well, we'll be using additional land," he says.

"From where, dear?" Margaret wants to know.

"The other family land," Wilbur says.

"What other family land, dear?" asks Margaret. "We don't have any other family land."

"The Square there," he replies sheepishly. "And the old building."

"What Square? What building?" she urges.

"You know," says Wilbur, "the . . . park there . . . and the old . . . church."

Margaret is stunned and raises her voice. "Wilbur! What are you saying?"

Jenny is alerted to the conversation. She turns down the radio and moves closer to the doorway to eavesdrop.

"It's just sitting there, Meg," Wilbur tries to explain. "Prime real estate right in the middle of town."

"You're using Cathedral Square for a shopping mall?" she shouts. "No, you're not! What about the Cathedral, Wilbur?"

"It's falling down," he replies without feeling.

"Falling down!" she exclaims. "Wilbur, your great-grandfather built that Cathedral!"

"They can't keep up the repairs," Wilbur counters.

THE EUCHARIST

"What do the twins say about this?" Margaret asks.

Wilbur does not respond.

"You didn't tell them, did you?"

Wilbur is silent.

Margaret is persistent. "Did you, Wilbur?"

Wilbur is noncommittal.

"Are you using their money?" she shouts.

"Meg, it's sitting there in a shoebox. They're gonna die and it'll go to the state unless it's invested in our land."

"You tricked them, didn't you!" she cries out. "You are not going to get away with this!"

"Meg, there are things about this that you don't understand," he retorts.

"Don't understand?" she screams, "Well, try me!"

"It's . . . confidential."

"Confidential?" Margaret shouts.

"There are legalities, Meg," argues Wilbur.

"Legalities!" repeats Margaret. "Is Pebblebaum in on this too? Why, you . . . " She storms from the room.

Jenny hears her mother coming, runs and quickly turns up the radio, then resumes ironing.

"Coming up next," states a radio announcer, "the news."

Margaret strides through the doorway. She passes by Jenny in a huff and keeps on walking straight into the hallway. "Men! Oh!" she mutters as she strides away. Jenny pretends not to hear, and turns her attention back to the radio.

"A rather unusual event took place at Mother of Sorrow Cathedral on Christmas Eve," states the news anchor. "During a telethon to raise money for the repair of the historic landmark, Father Michael Anthony, a young priest recently posted to the church, publicly advised the audience to not contribute to the restoration fund. The Cathedral received a whopping $65,000.00 from the telephone drive — more than enough to cover the repairs to the building, but almost all of it was pledged to meeting the needs of the poor."

"Way to go, Michael!" cries Jenny exuberantly.

"Father Anthony," the news anchor goes on, "also invited viewers to phone in if they needed assistance from the church. The Cathedral received more than 500 requests, ranging from Christmas turkeys to a date for the New Year's dance."

"Ha, ha! Good for you!" Jenny says with glee.

The news anchor continues. "When asked to explain, the priest replied, 'Let God look after the building. After all, He's the one who's writing the script'."

"Oh, Michael! You didn't!" Jenny mumbles to herself.

The news report continues. "Dean Potts, head of the Cathedral, confirmed today the young priest has been relieved of his duties."

THE EUCHARIST

"Oh, no!" Jenny cries out.

"Our broadcast news desk has also confirmed," the announcer continues, "that the aging building will be demolished to make way for a shopping centre."

"Oh, God!" cries Jenny. "And he will think I was in on it!" She unplugs the iron, runs to the closet, grabs her coat and rushes out the door.

CHAPTER XXI

In This Troubled World

Michael stands alone at the front of the Cathedral. He looks up at the stained-glass window. When he bows his head to pray, his doubts come flooding out.

In this troubled world I came to you
I thought you always knew just what to do
I knelt and prayed before your hallowed face
And now you've filled my spirit with disgrace

I followed where I thought your footsteps led
I listened carefully to what you said
I thought you cared that hungry mouths were fed
Where are you now

Michael turns and leaves from a side door. Moments later, Jenny enters the Cathedral and hurriedly walks up the centre aisle. "Michael?" she calls out. She stands at the communion rail and looks about. "Michael," she cries, "are you here?"

There is only silence. She peers to the sides and finds no one. She turns to leave, then pauses and looks up at the stained-glass window behind the altar. Now, in her own troubled world, she envisions Michael's state of mind and comes to his defense.

In his troubled world he came to you
He said you always knew just what to do
But now you've left him standing face to face
With emptiness and heartache and disgrace

He followed where he thought your footsteps led
He listened carefully to what you said
He thought you cared that hungry mouths were fed
Where are you now

Jenny walks back down the aisle of the sanctuary and leaves the Cathedral.

CHAPTER XXII

The Centre Enterprise

Wilbur sits in his second story office, surrounded by local businessmen. They are in a most celebratory mood, popping corks on bottles of champagne, congratulating Wilbur—and each other—on their lofty achievement.

"They raised a fortune . . . and can't use it to save the building!" gloats Wilbur.

"Talk about a gem!" says one man.

"It's too perfect!" says another.

"We're on our way, Wilbur!" offers a third.

"Poor Potts," utters Wilbur, "he's in a state. And that annoying little priest is out of the picture."

"Gotta give him credit for one thing," allows one of the men, "he made it easy for us."

"Couldn't have done it better if we had planned it ourselves," Wilbur agrees.

"You took a big gamble, Wilbur, and you won!" declares another businessman.

"Hear! Hear!" shout the men as they lift their glasses and drink to the beaming bank manager.

"And now for the prize," states Wilbur. He goes to his desk, pushes a button and speaks into his intercom. "Arnold, can you come in here." Almost instantaneously, there is a vigorous knock on the door.

"Yes, Arnold," Wilbur yells toward the door.

Arnold rushes in. He looks around at the merriment and breaks into a broad grin.

"Arnold," instructs Wilbur, "I want you to go over to the twins' place. There's a box there. A shoebox, actually. I want you to pick it up and bring it here."

"Yeth, thir," Arnold replies.

"Now they know you're coming," Wilbur continues. "You just go over there. Pick up the shoebox and come back here. Don't stop anywhere. Just go straight there and straight back."

"Yeth, thir," Arnold replies. "Thtraight there and thtraight back."

Wilbur picks up a canvas deposit bag. "Yes . . . and here, put the shoebox in this. And zip it up." He hands the canvas bag to Arnold.

"Put it in thith bag," Arnold reiterates. "And thip it up. Yeth, thir." He stands there.

"Okay, that's all," states Wilbur.

"Yeth, thir," Arnold repeats as he leaves the room.

Wilbur shouts after him, "And thtraight . . . I mean, straight back here."

THE EUCHARIST

"Yeth, thir. Thtraight back here," Arnold confirms from outside the office.

"All these years," Wilbur says to the businessmen, "they've kept their money in that shoebox!"

"Never could get 'em to put it in your bank, could ya!" says one of the men.

"Nope. Not 'til today!" Wilbur replies.

The men laugh and slap each other on the back. "Gentlemen," shouts one of them, "let's toast the Centre Enterprise!" They raise their glasses to a project of self-confessed underhandedness and launch into a series of one-line exchanges.

It's the blast-off for the cast-off of the Centre Enterprise

We didn't even have to take a loan
With mortgage rates that we cannot condone
And while we didn't cause a fuss
There are things we can't discuss
There'd be rumblings if the truth were ever known

All your shopping plaza pleasures will be met
There will even be a room where you can bet
Folks will come from miles aroun'
Spending money in our town
On the bargains that will help them go in debt

They hoot laughing and initiate another round of one-liners.

> *We'll have everything in everybody's size*
> *Fancy labels of imported merchandise*
> *There'll be ladies underwear*
> *And a parlor for their hair*
> *And a different kind of parlor for the guys*

"Hear! Hear!" the businessmen shout.

> *Oh, Spencer is the man that you can thank*
> *For elevating up your social rank*
> *You can look him in the eye*
> *With your head held high*
> *While he's stashing all your profits in his bank*

Wilbur breaks into a broad grin.

> *A clergyman will lay the cornerstone*
> *Will someone get the Bishop on the phone*
> *But we're gonna build it there on Cathedral Square*
> *So I think we'd better do it on our own*

They continue to congratulate each other and knock back champagne.

CHAPTER XXIII

Arnold and the 'Thoe Bokth'

Arnold hurries along Main Street with the bulging zipped deposit bag under his arm. He approaches the Spencer Department Store and notices Jenny fixing the kinetic display in the front window. Arnold pauses, and tries to get her attention with silent gestures through the thick glass.

The four delinquent boys, now back on the street, sneak up behind Arnold and, as a joke, grab the deposit bag from under his arm. Then they take off running and laughing down the street. Arnold feels for the bag. He panics, turns around and sees the four boys running, throwing the bag back and forth among themselves.

"Hey! Thtop!" shouts Arnold. He runs after them. "Thtop, you guyth." He puts his hands on his head. "I'm toatht!" he mutters to himself.

A police officer sees Arnold running and spots the chase. He starts running after the boys.

"Stop! Police!" the officer shouts.

Arnold stops short, and without looking behind him, throws his arms up in the air. "No, not you!" the policeman mutters as he runs past him.

Arnold puts his arms down and resumes running, struggling to keep up. The boys head down the street toward Cathedral Park. They see the policeman hot on their trail. One of them does a quick wind up and throws the bag at the bell on top of the wall.

Bullseye! The bell gongs!

Michael is standing beside the crèche on the other side of the wall. He looks up and sees the bag come flying toward him. It lands . . . right at his feet! The boys continue running. The policeman and Arnold, unaware of the drop, chase the boys right on by the Cathedral.

Michael stares at the bag. He looks up to the sky. Then he looks down at the bag again. He picks it up, opens it and discovers a shoebox filled with money! He looks up to the sky again. Then, holding the box of money in his hands, he stares bewildered at the crèche.

CHAPTER XXIV

Wilbur and the Sergeant

The telephone rings inside the police station. The Sergeant, sitting at his desk, picks up the receiver.

"Sergeant Hines here. . . . Who? . . . Catherine? And your last name? . . . Oh, the Spencer twin. That's your name, is it! . . . Yes, yes. How are you today? . . . Oh, just fine. . . . Yes, she's fine too. . . . A *what?* . . . No kidding! My goodness! . . . And it's all safely back? . . . The priest brought it? How'd he get it? . . . Well, that's really something. . . . No, I don't think so. Just a minute, I'll check." He holds his hand over the mouthpiece and shouts out the office door to the front counter. "Hey, Hank, anybody report a robbery this morning?"

"No sir," comes the policeman's reply.

"No, not yet," the Sergeant reports to the caller, and then listens. . . . "Oh, now, you sure you want me to do that? . . . Yeah, it would be a good lesson alright!" He starts to chuckle. . . . "Is that a fact! . . . And that's what that GEM business was all about. Didn't realize that. . . . Yeah, pretty tricky, alright! . . . Yeah, well look, you just leave it to me, then. . . . Yes, I'll proceed as if it's still missing. . . . Don't you worry about that. I'll handle it myself. . . . Okay, now, good-b—"

The Sergeant starts to hang up the receiver. The caller says something else.

"What's that? . . . Well, we wouldn't want people to think he was in on it. . . . Ah, I get your point. Okay, I won't tell 'em. I'll let them go lookin' for 'im. . . . Well, how about you just keep him there 'cause that's the last place they're gonna look. . . . What's that? . . . He can tell you apart, can he! That's really something! . . . And he gets it right every time, well, well. . . . Yeah, I guess you could call that a miracle. . . . Okay, now, good-bye."

The Sergeant hangs up the telephone, grins with satisfaction, and then chuckles out loud. He gets up from his desk and walks to the doorway leading to the main office. "Hank," he says, "the bank manager should be showing up any minute now. When he comes, let me handle it."

"Okay, sir," the police officer responds.

A scene of pandemonium breaks out as Wilbur, with Arnold in tow, pounces into the police station. Wilbur is panicking. "A robbery!" he shouts frantically. "There's been a robbery!"

The Sergeant gets up from his desk and walks to the front counter. "At the bank, sir?"

THE EUCHARIST

"No, not the bank," shouts Wilbur. "On the street!"

"From you, sir?" says the Sergeant.

"No, no, not from me. From Arnold here."

The Sergeant turns to Arnold. "You were robbed, sir?"

"Yeth, thir," Arnold replies.

"Who robbed you, Arnold?" the Sergeant asks.

"Thum boyth, thir."

"Who?" the Sergeant asks again.

"Those delinquent punks," shouts Wilbur. "Those no good—"

"And what did they take?" the Sergeant asks.

"A thoe bokth," says Arnold.

"A what?" the Sergeant says.

"Thoe bokth," repeats Arnold.

The Sergeant looks at him. "Thoe bokth?"

"A shoebox," interrupts Wilbur. "Never mind that. Money! They took money!"

"Money . . . in a shoebox?" the Sergeant questions.

"Yes!" cries Wilbur, "The entire family fortune! In a shoebox!"

Arnold is shocked to learn it is the Spencer fortune. He gasps, and puts his hands on his forehead. "Holy thufferin'!"

The Sergeant lifts his eyebrows, then continues filling out a report. "Okay. And how much money did they take?"

"Don't know, thir," replies Arnold.

"You don't know?" says the Sergeant.

"No, thir. It wath in the thoe bokth, I gueth." Arnold tries to explain.

The Sergeant pretends he is struggling to get the story straight. "You guess? You don't know if there was money in the thoe . . . I mean, shoebox?"

Arnold is getting flustered. "I jutht went thtraight there and thtraight back."

"Thraight there and thtraight back . . . Okay, let's start again. Who was robbed?" says the Sergeant.

Wilbur points to Arnold. "He was . . . well, I was."

The Sergeant sighs and raises his eyebrows again.

"I wath, sir," sputters Arnold. "No." He points to Wilbur. "He wath . . . I guethth we both wath." He waves his arms about, trying to clarify the situation.

"Okay," the Sergeant begins again, "who had the money?"

"Me, thir, in a thoe bokth," Arnold says.

"You had the money in a shoebox," the Sergeant confirms. "It was your money?"

"No, thir," says Arnold, "wathn't my money."

"Okay," the Sergeant responds. He points to Wilbur. "It was his money?"

"No, thir," says Arnold, "wathn't hith money."

THE EUCHARIST

The Sergeant pretends exasperation. "It wasn't your money and it wasn't his money. Okay, then, whose money was it, Arnold?"

"Thpenther thithters," Arnold replies.

The Sergeant leans forward. "Whose?"

"The Spencer sisters," shouts Wilbur, impatiently. "The twins, darn it."

The Sergeant looks into Arnold's eyes. "Let me get this straight. You had the twins' money, Arnold?"

"Yeth, thir, in a thoe bokth," he says.

"I know, in a 'thoe bokth'," repeats the Sergeant. "Now, what were you doing with their money, Arnold?"

"Taking it thtraight to Mithter Thpenther," Arnold explains.

"To?" the Sergeant asks again.

"To the bank, darn it!" shouts Wilbur. "To deposit it in the bank!"

"Arnold was depositing somebody else's money in your bank, Wilbur?" questions the Sergeant.

"Yes, yes," says Wilbur, "Arnold was depositing—"

The Sergeant interrupts and turns to Arnold. "You had their written authorization to do this?"

Arnold is confused. He leans forward. "Thorry?"

"He was on banking duty," explains Wilbur. "I sent him."

The Sergeant looks at Wilbur. "Ah, I see. So you had the written authorization."

"Well, not exactly in writing," says Wilbur.

"You took money without written authorization?" the Sergeant asks Wilbur.

"Never mind that," says Wilbur. "It'll all be done in due course."

"Well," states the Sergeant, "I'm afraid we've got a bit of a problem here. You see, you and your bank, Wilbur, are liable for any missing funds unless you have authorization in writing from the owners to remove the monies from their domicile."

"Now, you just wait a minute . . ." Wilbur protests.

The Sergeant continues. "You, Wilbur, are asking the authorities to believe that somebody took the money from you that you took from somebody else."

"Those delinquent punks out there stole it!" cries Wilbur.

"As far as I'm concerned," the Sergeant declares with an air of seriousness, "if you took unauthorized money, sir, you are the one responsible for it. I think you had better pay a visit to your lawyer."

A look of shock comes over Wilbur's face. He stares at the Sergeant who maintains a stoic expression. Wilbur grabs Arnold by the arm and drags him out of the room in a fury.

When the two men are out of sight, the Sergeant throws back his head and laughs.

CHAPTER XXV

Verger and the Officer Again

The Verger is alone inside the Cathedral, sweeping and dusting the area around the altar. A police officer barges in, pulling one of the delinquent boys by the collar. "Okay," shouts the policeman, "where is he?"

"What seems to be the problem, Officer?" the Verger replies calmly.

"C'mon, don't play dumb," he says to the Verger. "Where is he?"

"Where is who, sir?" the Verger asks.

"The priest! The priest! C'mon!" The policeman is impatient.

"He is no longer with us, sir," the Verger explains.

"You in on it, too?" yells the policeman.

"In on what, sir?" asks the Verger.

"C'mon, it's all over town," the policeman yells. "Where's he hiding?"

The young boy turns to the policeman. "He didn't know anything about it. It was just a joke. We were teasing the nerd."

"These punks made a drop to the priest," announces the policeman.

The Verger tries to respond. "Ah, sir, that doesn't sound like—"

"Don't be stupid!" the policeman interrupts. "Just figure it out. He plans a telethon to tell people they need a big chunk of money to save the Cathedral. Then he tells the people not to give money to save the Cathedral. Why? Because he had the whole thing planned. He comes off a big hero. Doin' miracles. Playin' God."

"Nothing was planned, I tell you," the boy tries to explain. "He just happened to be there."

The policeman retorts. "Shut up, punk, or I'll—"

"Hold on a minute, sir," interrupts the Verger.

The youth explains to the Verger this time. "We threw it at the bell on top of the wall. We didn't know it was money. It was just a joke."

"I have a warrant for the arrest of Father Michael Anthony," states the policeman. "Would you know his whereabouts?"

"Well, like I said, sir," responds the Verger, "he is no longer with us."

"You could be in serious trouble, old man," the policeman states, "for harboring a criminal." He turns to leave with the youth.

"What about the boy, sir?" the Verger asks.

THE EUCHARIST

"Mark, my word, he's pulled his last heist in this town," states the policeman. "The rest of his gang, too."

"We were just havin' fun with the nerd," the boy tries one last time to explain.

"They're only children, sir. Nothing better to do," offers the Verger. "How about we make a plan for—"

"Not goin' to fall for that one again," the policeman retorts. "This time they're goin' to a place they won't soon forget."

The officer leaves, dragging the youth by the collar. The Verger watches with sadness as the boy looks back at him. He thinks of his poem again.

If God is love then what is hate about
It comes from watching us
That children sort the answer out
For some to go on living
Seems that others have to die
Oh, how long will children keep on caring why

CHAPTER XXVI

Jenny and the Revelation

Jenny returns to the Cathedral. She finds the Verger cleaning inside the sanctuary.

"Do you know where I can find Michael?" she asks.

"He's gone, I'm afraid," replies the Verger.

"I've got to find him," says Jenny. "He'll think I was part of it."

"I don't think so, Jenny," the Verger says softly.

"No, some of the things I said," she explains. "It's like I was setting him up."

"Oh, I think he knows how it is," he tells her in a comforting voice.

"But there's . . . oh, I must see him," she goes on. "Where could he be?"

"I don't know," the Verger replies, "but I expect he'll leave on the Sunday train. You could go down to the station."

"They don't realize what they've done," she says.

"No, he's very special. I'll miss him," the Verger responds.

"He'll miss you too," says Jenny. "He liked you. Like when he figured out the pure virgin and the mother of sorrow were the same woman, he had to run and tell you right away. I couldn't believe he didn't—"

"He told you?" the Verger interrupts.

"I already knew," Jenny replies.

"That's why he brought me here."

"Who?" asks Jenny.

"Your great-great-grandfather."

Jenny is getting confused. "What?" she asks.

"She was my mother," says the Verger.

"Who was your mother?" Jenny is now thoroughly confused.

"Catherine . . . the one who died."

"What are you talking about?" exclaims Jenny.

"Catherine and Dolores," the Verger replies. "That's what Michael figured out. They're the same person. The twins are named after her.

"The twins? You mean my great-aunties?"

"Yes, Jenny," reveals the Verger. "Your great-great-grandfather had a daughter named Catherine. She got pregnant very young, and her father sent her away. She went to a home to have the baby. She didn't want to disgrace the family so she never told them her name. The nuns called her Dolores . . . mother of sorrow . . . because she was so sad."

THE EUCHARIST

Jenny grows pensive. "Oh . . . that's what he meant when . . ."

"She died soon after I was born," the Verger relates. "Grand-dad kept it all a secret, but he built this Cathedral as a memorial to her. Everyone thinks it's named after Mary, mother of Jesus."

Jenny starts to cry. "Oh, he was trying to save the Cathedral and I . . ."

"Don't fret about it," says the Verger. "Everything will work out."

"But it's all over," Jenny cries.

"No, not over," states the Verger, "because there is something deep inside that the world cannot touch. And when we approach that inner realm, we cannot have the last word. You see, Jenny, the world of matter and the world of spirit are identical twins. This is the mystery of our being. . . . Now you stay here as long as you like. I'm going to finish cleaning up my mother's house." He pats her on the shoulder and resumes his work.

Jenny stands there, tears welling in her eyes. "Oh, Michael . . . where *are* you?" she cries. She stares up at the stained-glass window of the mother with the infant child. It means something so different to her now. She kneels down at the communion rail and makes her petition, using many of the same words she has come to know as Michael's prayer.

In my troubled world I come to you
He said you always know just what to do
For now I feel an emptiness within
Like something new is trying to begin

I ask your guidance starting from today
I ask your wisdom to know what to say
I ask your footprints so I'll find the way
Please hear me now

Jenny gets up from the communion rail. She looks once more at the stained-glass window. "Oh, Michael, I love you," she declares. Then she turns, walks down the aisle and leaves.

CHAPTER XXVII

Wilbur and the Twins Again

It is Sunday morning. Wilbur sits in his armchair in the living room. Margaret is uncharacteristically calm as the doorbell rings. *"Ding, ding! Ding, ding! Ding, ding!"*

"Good Lord, it's the twins!" exclaims Wilbur. "Meg, tell them I'm not here. Say I've gone to church or something."

Margaret points her finger at him. "Wilbur, you sit right there. Don't move, I tell you." She opens the door.

Catherine and Dolores step inside. For the first time, they appear very distinct from each other. They wear different styles, different colors, even display different gestures and mannerisms.

"Aunties, come right in," says Margaret. "So good to see you. Don't you look lovely!" She raises her voice. "Wilbur, dear, look who's come to visit." Then she turns back to the twins. "Come right this way."

Catherine and Dolores march into the living room. "Hello, Wilbur," says Catherine.

"How are you, nephew?" adds Dolores.

Wilbur does a double take and shuffles nervously in his seat. "Aunties . . . how nice to . . . won't you . . . how are we today?"

Dolores takes the lead this time. "Well, we're a little pissed off, Wilbur."

"We hear our money's missing," adds Catherine.

Wilbur is shaken. He struggles to regain composure. "Yes, those delinquent punks," he responds nervously. "They grabbed it from Arnold. Don't worry, we'll get it back."

"Well, that's another thing, Wilbur," Dolores pipes up again. "What were you planning to do with it when you got it back?"

"Well . . . Aunties . . . the development," says Wilbur. "You know . . . the plans I showed you. Remember?"

"Oh yes, the plans," says Catherine. "I think there's something you forgot to include in that, Wilbur."

"Oh, let me see now . . . I'm trying to remember . . ." He fidgets. "Ummm . . . what might that be?"

"The location, perhaps?" states Dolores.

"Oh, didn't I tell you that?" Wilbur answers. "Ah, maybe that was it. Ah, yes, well . . . ummm, I was planning to go over that with you when everything was in place."

"Yes, I just bet you were," replies Dolores.

"Well, don't you worry; we'll do that." Wilbur thinks he's out of the woods.

THE EUCHARIST

"Well, Wilbur, dear," says Catherine, "seems there's another problem."

"Whatever it is, I'm sure we can fix it." Wilbur tries to appear innocent and confident.

"Yes, I'm sure we can," Catherine retorts.

"It's about the Cathedral, nephew," states Dolores.

"Ah, yes, the Cathedral," replies Wilbur, "I'm afraid the young priest made a mess of that."

"Did he now," states Dolores.

"We want the Cathedral repaired, Wilbur," states Catherine.

"Well, they didn't raise the funds for that," replies Wilbur in a matter-of-fact manner.

"And the priest reinstated, nephew," adds Dolores.

Wilbur is aghast. "I can't do that! The Dean fired him!"

"The Cathedral repaired, Wilbur," states Catherine firmly.

"And the priest reinstated," adds Dolores more firmly still.

"Now, Aunties . . ." Wilbur tries to reason with them.

"Do it, nephew," instructs Dolores.

Wilbur appeals to his wife. "Meg, can you explain to them that . . ."

"No, I can't, Wilbur."

"Oh, and there's one more thing," adds Catherine.

Wilbur is getting weaker by the moment. "More?" he moans.

"We didn't authorize the bank to take our money," she replies.

Wilbur is feeling trapped. "Now, Aunties, I set it up with you. We talked on the telephone, remember? I said I would send Arnold over and I told you . . ."

"It looks to the police like you stole our money," states Dolores.

Wilbur realizes he is playing a losing game. "Oh, Lord!" he mutters.

"Unless you have our signed authorization," states Catherine, "the police will charge you with robbery."

"Do you realize that, nephew?" pipes up Dolores.

"Meg," pleads Wilbur, "can you—"

"You're on your own, Wilbur," Margaret responds.

Wilbur fidgets nervously.

"So I guess you'd better get it," Catherine continues.

Wilbur is defeated. "Okay," he concedes, "what do I have to do?"

"Can you witness our signatures, Wilbur?" Dolores asks, knowing full well he cannot tell them apart.

"Oh, Lord!" he grumbles.

"No, you can't," she adds. "Nobody can except . . ."

"Guess who, nephew," taunts Catherine.

"Oh, not that annoying little priest," Wilbur utters in frustration.

THE EUCHARIST

"Yes, Wilbur, that annoying little priest," Catherine repeats. "And you had better get him here to witness our signatures or we'll allow the police to charge you with robbery."

"And you better get the Dean to hire him back or we won't sign," adds Dolores.

"Oh, Lord!" cries Wilbur.

"Is that clear, nephew?" asks Dolores.

Wilbur runs his hands through his hair in despair. "Lord, oh Lord!"

The twins stand up and prepare to leave. Wilbur starts to get up to see them out.

"Oh, don't get up, Wilbur," states Catherine. "Save your energy. You're going to need every bit of it."

Margaret ushers the twins to the door. They give each other the thumbs up and chuckle. Catherine and Dolores leave.

Margaret closes the door and walks back into the living room. "Well, Wilbur?" she says, firmly.

Wilbur sighs and wrings his hands.

"Better get on with it," she continues.

Wilbur remains seated and mutters in a confused state. "How in heaven's name am I supposed to—"

"Heaven's name is right," Margaret retorts. "Start with the Dean, I think."

"I can't tell the Dean to—"

"Better hurry, Wilbur," she interrupts. "The train will be leaving in less than an hour."

"But it's Sunday, Meg," he protests. "The Dean's at Eucharist."

"Then that's where you'll find him," replies Margaret without even a smidgeon of empathy.

Wilbur pulls at his hair in despair again. "Lord, oh Lord, oh Lord!" he mumbles to himself.

"Better get going, Wilbur," urges Margaret. "No time to lose." She hands him his coat and ushers him to the door.

A muddled Wilbur reluctantly but hastily leaves.

CHAPTER XXVIII

The Priest and Wilbur Again

Dean Potts is officiating at the Sunday Eucharist. The church is now overflowing with a motley group of new communicants enticed by the telethon. The Dean serves the bread and wine as the choir sings.

> *Jesus like a shepherd lead us*
> *Turn us from our selfish ways*
> *Take our hearts and gently feed us*
> *Nurture us through all our days*
> *Guide our hand when we are strong*
> *Understand when we are wrong*
> *Let us evermore to be*
> *In thy blessed company*

Wilbur enters the Cathedral and steals his way to the front of the sanctuary. Then he pushes to the front of the communion line, partially kneeling at the railing.

Dean Potts moves along the railing, administering the sacraments. Wilbur tries to get his attention.

"Pssst!" Wilbur gestures through partially closed lips.

The Dean continues in his ritual mode, serving the kneeling communicants. Wilbur tries again, a bit louder this time. "Pssst! Potts!" he says.

Dean Potts notices him this time. Wilbur beckons the Dean to skip the line at the railing and come directly to him. "Get over here!" he whispers.

The Dean stares at him. Then he points to the line. Wilbur shakes his head. "Over here! Hurry!" he gestures.

Dean Potts looks around, then slips over to Wilbur. The puzzled communicants stare to see what is going on.

"Gotta get the priest back," states Wilbur.

"What?" the Dean responds.

"Anthony Michael . . . or whatever his name is," utters a muddled Wilbur. "Need him back."

"Talk to me after," the Dean says as he points to the line of waiting communicants.

"No time," Wilbur exclaims. "You've got to come to the station now."

The communicants grow curious and try to figure out what is going on.

Dean Potts tries to restore some order. "Wilbur," he urges, "you're interrupting the—"

"If the priest goes, you go!" Wilbur says adamantly.

Dean Potts does a quick take, and thrusts the plate at a kneeling communicant. "Here! Pass this around, will

THE EUCHARIST

you," he instructs. The communicant holds the plate, not knowing what to do with it.

Dean Potts gulps down the remaining wine and plunks the cup on the altar. He beckons Wilbur off to the side. The two of them engage in animated conversation. The Dean reacts with shock.

The Eucharist comes to a halt. The communicants start whispering to each other.

"It's about the priest," says one of them.

"They're gonna get him back," whispers another.

Dean Potts and Wilbur rush down the central aisle of the Cathedral. The choir members stare for a moment, look at each other, then head down the aisle behind them. The communicants follow in pursuit. Everyone rushes out the front door of the Cathedral—everyone except the Verger, that is, who quietly watches them go.

CHAPTER XXIX

Lord, Have Mercy!

Down at the railway station, the train sits on the platform. Its departure bell sounds as the final boarding announcement peels over the loud speaker. "Last call for Cambridge and all points south to London. All aboard!"

Michael, luggage in hand, boards the train just ahead of the pursuing entourage that floods onto the platform. Wilbur is in hot pursuit, followed by Dean Potts in clerical robe, the choir members—still in their gowns—and a motley collection of the congregation.

Wilbur rushes up to the ticket window. "Got a priest on board?" he shouts to the ticket agent.

"You need a priest, sir?" the ticket agent replies.

"No, no," he explains, "did you sell a ticket to a . . . you know . . . dog collar?" He points to his neck.

Dean Potts gives the bank manager a disapproving glance. Wilbur catches on. "Sorry," he says to the Dean and turns his attention back to the ticket agent. "Did you sell one to a priest?"

The ticket agent answers slowly. "Yes, now, seems to me I did."

"He's on board?" Wilbur urges.

"Should be by now," the ticket agent affirms.

"Well, hold the train!" Wilbur shouts at him.

"Afraid I can't do that, sir," the agent replies without emotion, "but it's still on the platform."

Wilbur rushes from the ticket window, pulling Dean Potts with him. He gazes down the platform into the row of coaches, frantically checking one, then the next. Then he spots Michael sitting by an open window.

"There he is!" Wilbur shouts. Dean Potts looks in the direction of Wilbur's pointing finger.

Wilbur prods the Dean. "Tell him!" Wilbur instructs.

Dean Potts struggles along the platform. "Michael, hold on a minute," the Dean shouts.

Michael looks out the window and sees them.

"Get off the train," the Dean continues.

"What for?" Michael shouts back.

"You've got your job back," states the Dean.

"I quit, remember?" Michael responds.

Dean Potts looks at Wilbur and shrugs. "He quit, remember?"

"Well, unquit him!" shouts Wilbur, waving his arms. "Just get him back."

"We want you back, Michael," the Dean mutters apologetically.

THE EUCHARIST

"Sorry. Not my thing," Michael replies.

Wilbur pushes Dean Potts out of the way and makes his plea directly. "Cathedral stays, son," he shouts.

Michael does not respond.

"We're gonna repair it, son," Wilbur continues.

"Too late," says Michael.

"Run any program you want, son," pleads Wilbur.

Dean Potts glares at Wilbur. Wilbur glances back. "Sorry," he says to the Dean and turns back to Michael. "Whatever you need, son..."

Michael remains firm. "No," he states, "and it's not 'son'—it's 'Father'."

The whistle blows. The train is about to leave the platform. Wilbur is beside himself. He looks around in desperation. Just then he spots his wife and daughters running onto the platform, along with Catherine and Dolores, followed by the police Sergeant and the four delinquent boys.

Wilbur makes one last effort. "I beg you," he pleads to Michael. No response. Wilbur looks back at his family and shouts to them. "Meg, do something!" he cries out.

"It's not Meg. It's Margaret, dear," says his wife.

"Angel," Wilbur pleads, "please tell your mother—"

"My name is Angelina," she replies, aware that her mother is angry with her husband because he reversed her nickname to conjure up his deception.

"Jenny?" he pleads.

Jenny throws her support to her mother. "It's not Jenny, father. It's Jennifer," she replies.

Wilbur looks to his one remaining daughter, begging for her help. "Priscilla—"

"Doesn't have a nickname!" Priscilla retorts.

Wilbur stops short. He stands motionless in a state of frenzy. "Lord, have mercy!" he cries out.

"Not here, Wilbur," replies an uncomfortable Dean Potts.

The train jerks and slowly begins to move forward. Wilbur looks back at Michael sitting in the coach and clasps his hands together. He is desperate.

"Pleeeease, I beg you!" he cries out to Michael.

Michael spots Jenny standing on the platform. He leans out the open window. "On one condition," he shouts back to Wilbur.

Wilbur trots down the platform to keep within speaking range of the moving train. "Anything! Just name it!" Wilbur responds, sensing a breakthrough at last.

Michael looks past Wilbur and straight at Jenny. "Jenny," he shouts, "will you marry me?"

The crowd hushes. Jenny stands motionless. Wilbur puts his hands on his head in disbelief. "Oh, Lord, have mercy!" he exclaims.

Dean Potts clenches his teeth. "I said not here, Wilbur!"

THE EUCHARIST

Jenny looks at Michael. She is stunned and tries to catch her breath.

The train inches forward.

Jenny looks at her father. He is aghast! She takes a measure of delight in his predicament. She looks around, clasps her hands to her chest, grabs a breath and looks back at Michael. There is a pregnant pause.

"Yes!" Jenny shouts.

The crowd cheers. "Stop the train! Stop the train!" people shout.

The train jerks to a grinding halt. The steam brakes hiss. Wilbur falls to his knees on the platform and puts his head in his hands. "Lord! Oh Lord! Oh Lord!" he cries out. Dean Potts stares down at him—but this time he says nothing.

Michael alights from the train. Jenny pushes through the crowd and makes her way down the platform. The crowd clears a path for them.

Michael and Jenny meet. They fall into each other's arms, and kiss passionately.

The crowd goes wild!

Wilbur sobs.

CHAPTER XXX

Michael and Jenny . . . forever

Jenny and Michael stand before the altar of the Cathedral at the celebration of their wedding. Dean Potts officiates. The choir sings.

In this troubled world they come to you
You always seem to know just what to do
So now they kneel before your hallowed face
To still their minds and fill their souls with grace

They ask your guidance on this special day
They ask your footprints so they'll find the way
They ask your wisdom to know what to say
Please hear them now

When the vows are completed, the couple walks joyously together down the centre aisle. They stand on the front steps of the Cathedral as wedding guests cluster around them.

The chatter of the excited guests is interrupted by the honk of a car horn. All eyes turn in the direction of the sound to see the four delinquent boys drive up in a rental car decorated with ribbons and a "Just Married" sign. A policeman pretends to go after them.

Everyone laughs.

The delinquent boys get out of the car and throw the keys to Arnold who, in turn, tosses them to Michael. Arnold has rented the car for the couple's honeymoon!

Everyone cheers.

Jenny turns her back to the crowd to throw her bouquet. The women cluster together on the steps below her. The distinctly and smartly dressed Catherine and Dolores join the women. Jenny throws the bouquet. Dolores leaps into the air and catches the flowers. With bouquet in hand, she turns to Dean Potts who quickly shies away. Then she turns to Arnold who jokingly returns the smile with pretence of interest.

Everyone laughs and cheers.

The bridal party stands on the steps of the Cathedral for one last wedding photo. Wilbur gives Jenny a hug. Then he slaps Michael on the back. "I've got to hand it to you, Father," he says to the priest.

Michael turns to Wilbur, "Actually," he says, "it's not 'Father' — it's 'son'!"

Wilbur throws his arms in the air. "A son! I have a son!" he exclaims as the camera clicks.

EPILOGUE

The Alpha and the Omega

Like all the years before and all that would be hence, the Christmas season comes to an end this year. And when it is time to dismantle the nativity scene, once again the Verger walks over to the crèche and looks at the statuette of Mary. "Ah," he whispers to her softly, "do I detect a faint smile on your face, dear mother? Yes, you worked your little miracle again this year." He picks up the statuette and carries it gently inside the Cathedral.

A Cathedral endowed with new life, to be sure. For a photograph in a church bulletin the following year shows Michael with a very pregnant Jenny, standing in front of the old building surrounded by scaffolding.

In another photograph a few years hence, the couple is standing at a ribbon-cutting ceremony in front of the newly renovated Cathedral. But this time they do not stand alone. Beside them are two little girls . . . Michael and Jenny have twins!

ABOUT THE AUTHOR

Pamela J Peck is an author, lecturer, composer and playwright whose professional interest is education for a global perspective, and the application of social science knowledge to the practical concerns of everyday life. Canadian born, she holds the degrees of Bachelor of Arts in Psychology and Religion (Mount Allison University), Bachelor of Social Work, Master of Social Work and PhD in Anthropology (UBC). She was a Research Associate at the University of Delhi in India and a Research Fellow at the University of the South Pacific in Fiji.

Pamela has traveled to more than eighty countries around the world, and has lived and studied in many of them. She uses her research and experience to infuse and inform her novels, short stories, screenplays and stage musicals. Drawing on the archetypal structure of classical mythology and Jungian psychology, her creative works embody timeless and universal principles. Her stories appeal to people of all ages as she takes us on magical and adventurous journeys to the far corners of the outer world, and into the inner recesses of the human mind.

The Eucharist
STAGE MUSICAL

The Eucharist was originally written as a musical stage play. Some of the musical numbers in the stage version do not appear in the storybook edition. The Eucharist is one of five major musicals by composer/playwright Pamela J Peck.

Information on this and other stage and screen projects will be found on the *PJ Productions* website,

www.pjproductions.ca.

Information on the author Pamela J Peck will be found on the Author website,

www.pamelajpeck.com.

PJ Productions

PJ Productions is an artistic company with office in Vancouver, Canada. Founded by composer/playwright Pamela J Peck and journalist Ken Johnson, it looks to the artist as leader, and seeks association with like-minded individuals and companies whose practices are congruent with its mission.

MISSION STATEMENT

To create and develop outstanding projects that enrich, enlighten and entertain creators and audiences alike.

ISBN 142513102-6